KINGDUMB

by Jonathan Cook

GHOST LIGHT

PUBLICATIONS

KINGDUMB

SPECIAL NOTE

Anyone receiving permission to produce KINGDUMB is required to give credit to the Author as sole and exclusive Author of the Play on the title page of all programs distributed in connection with performances of the Play and in all instances in which the title of the Play appears for purposes of advertising, publicizing or otherwise exploiting the Play and/or a production thereof. The name of the Author must appear on a separate line, in which no other name appears, immediately beneath the title and in size of type equal to 50% of the size of the largest, most prominent letter used for the title of the Play. No person, firm, or entity may receive credit larger or more prominent than that accorded the Author.

SPECIAL NOTE ON SONGS AND RECORDINGS

For performances of copyrighted songs, arrangements or recordings mentioned in these Plays, the permission of the copyright owner(s) must be obtained. Other songs, arrangements or recordings may be substituted provided permission from the copyright owner(s) of such songs, arrangements or recordings is obtained; or songs, arrangements or recordings in the public domain may be substituted.

Book & Cover Design: Jonathan Cook
First Edition: March 2024
ISBN 978-1-964045-01-6

"It's good to be the King."
– Mel Brooks

KINGDUMB received its premiere at Le Chat Noir Theatre in Augusta, GA on October 21, 2023 as part of a live audio play recording for the Gather by the Ghost Light podcast. It was directed by Jonathan Cook; the foley effects by TJ McSherry; and with audio engineer Nick Laws. The cast was as follows:

CORBIN MOSS .... Julian Diaz
CAYLY MOSS .... Marian Thibodeau
OSWALDO MOSS ....Luke Romagnoli
HENRI HACKUS .... Devon McSherry
RICHARD TAXMAN .... Brandon Dawson
KING AMADO .... Michael Silvio Fortino
LEON .... Krys Bailey
DEKE HARVEY .... Robb Smith
D. DUNCAN .... Adam Cowart
ESTELLE AVERY .... Arelis Rivera
GUARD BELLYWAX .... Jonathan Cook
GUARD HERMAN .... Chelsea Glass
JEREMY THE SAGE .... Eric Odom
LENNY THE DRAGON SLAYER .... Karla Fischbach
DOBSON .... Eric Odom
KINGDOM PRESS COURIER .... Karla Fischbach

KINGDUMB

CHARACTERS

CORBIN
Male, 30-40's; Husband of Cayly and father to Oswaldo. The region's finest clock fixer, aka "Time Repair Specialist".

CAYLY
Female, 30-40's; Wife of Corbin and mother to Oswaldo.

OSWALDO
Male, Teenager; Home-schooled son of Corbin and Cayly.

HENRI
Female, any adult age; Best friend and neighbor to Corbin and Cayly. Has a tendency to get nervous about every little thing.

ESTELLE
Female, 20-30's; Journalist for the Kingdom Press.

DEKE HARVEY
Male, any adult age; Smooth talking insurance salesman who is skilled in the art of "Sensatone". This by definition is described as being able to make anything you say appear to make sense no matter how absurd the comment may be.

D. DUNCAN
Male, any adult age; The local law librarian.

KING AMADO
Male, 20-30's; The new King of the land.

LEON
Male, any adult age; King Amado's court jester.

RICHARD TAXMAN
*Male, any adult age; The Kingdom tax collector. *His last name is NOT pronounced as "Tax Man". It's all one word, like Silverman, Coleman, or Human.*

JEREMY THE SAGE
Male, any adult age; Sibling of Lenny. Not really a sage. Just a really good guesser.

LENNY
Female, any adult age; Sibling of Jeremy the Sage and commonly titled Lenny the Dragon Slayer.

DOBSON
Male, any adult age; A Kingdom resident that mysteriously vanished one day after not being able to pay taxes.

GUARD BELLYWAX
Any gender, any adult age; Member of King Amado's Royal Guard.

GUARD HERMAN
Any gender, any adult age; Member of King Amado's Royal Guard.

COURIER
Any gender, any age. Delivers the Kingdom Press newsletter.

CASTING NOTE: Jeremy, Lenny, Dobson, the Guards, and the courier all have smaller roles for potential doubling if needed.

SPECIAL NOTE: Producing theatres have permission to change genders for any of the characters.

PLACE

A fictional kingdom full of fictional characters that doesn't exist, nor will it ever.

TIME

Medieval times. Somewhere around the moment Jimmy the Harp first learned to tie his shoes, give or take a decade.

ACT ONE
Scene 1

Afternoon. The main room of a medieval-style home. It's clean in the sense that most things are in their place, however, there's an unusually vast supply of clocks and pocket watches lying about.

At rise, Cayly and her teenage son, Oswaldo, sit at a table in the room. They're going over their daily home-schooling routine. Oswaldo seems to be getting bored, but Cayly pushes on because she knows her son needs an education.

CAYLY. Come on, Oz. Do you know the answer? We just went over this yesterday. Who was the bard that started the Treebobber Alliance?

OSWALDO. Ummm … was it Vincent Haven?

CAYLY. Yes! I knew you were listening!

OSWALDO. *(Annoyed.)* Mom, can we please switch to another subject? I can't handle any more history questions.

CAYLY. Only a few more pages til we're done with the chapter quiz. Now, tell me which Commander won the Battle of Everless?

OSWALDO. Mom, please.

CAYLY. I'll give you a hint. He wore an eye patch and his name rhymes with Scary Buckenberry.

OSWALDO. What's the point in learning about something

that's already happened?

CAYLY. What's the point? These are historical events. They helped establish our society and ... our culture.

OSWALDO. Well, if these things happened years ago, why should I care?

CAYLY. Just understand that history is something that's beneficial for everyone to learn. There have been great achievements that have happened in the past as well as terrible mistakes. Learning about these past events and people enables us to take that knowledge and prepare for things to come. For example, if you went running through a forest and you fell into a ditch that was filled with vile and venomous snakes, you would know never to run that direction in the forest again, right?

OSWALDO. And I'd be dead.

CAYLY. But the people that read about what happened to you will know how you died and they will learn from your mistake. They'll know never to trot down that particular path. Does any of that make sense?

OSWALDO. So, you're saying that studying history is all about people in the present benefiting from the misfortune of people in the past?

CAYLY. To an extent I guess, but not entirely. It can also inspire you to achieve goals. Think about all those inventors and even the artists you've read about. They all inspire today's generation.

OSWALDO. It still doesn't explain why I need to know which bard started the Treebobber Alliance.

CAYLY. Okay. I give up. That's enough history for today. Let's just move on to the next subject.

OSWALDO. Thank you!

CAYLY. *(Looks through other textbooks on the table.)* Ah. Here we go. If history is boring you, then how bout we dive into this next subject instead – The Future!

OSWALDO. Ugh! Like that's any better!

CAYLY. What's the problem?

OSWALDO. Why is "The Future" a school subject?

CAYLY. It just is! There's no history without a future. Now, I'm not going to waste time explaining why each subject is essential. They're all part of the curriculum and I'm required to teach you all of them.

OSWALDO. *(Giving up.)* Fine.

CAYLY. Let's see. Last time, we finished up chapter four - The Bright Ages. So, begin today reading chapter seven - The Prosperous Fool.

OSWALDO. Why are we skipping chapters five and six?

CAYLY. When studying the future, it's good to practice doing future activities in the present, like reading a chapter in your book that you planned on reading at a later date. You'll get a better understanding of the subject.

OSWALDO. That makes no sense whatsoever.

CAYLY. Just read! *(Oswaldo begins reading.)* Look. I know I'm not very good at this. But your education is important and if I had known I was going to have to teach you myself this year, I would have prepared better. We weren't given any warning that the schools were reaching max capacity.

OSWALDO. I don't want you to feel that way. It's not your fault.

CAYLY. This teaching thing is tough, but I'm not going to let you get behind just because they said there was no room for you. I'll get better. I promise.

OSWALDO. It's fine, Mom. A lot of my friends are going through this same thing right now. I'm not the only one whose parents have had to do what you're doing.

CAYLY. Hey … that gives me an idea. Maybe we can have a joint study group with some of the other kids your age.

How about I ask the Sinclair's if they'll start bringing their daughter Stacy to our lessons? They live only two houses down and you're both at the same level. What do you think?

OSWALDO. I don't know. She's kinda mean. And she has a pet rat that she shaved her name into its fur. That's just weird.

CAYLY. I'm sure she's not that bad. I'll invite her over next week. *(Knocking is heard at the front door.)* Oh, who could that be? *(She opens the door and sees the Kingdom Press Courier.)*

COURIER. Good afternoon, Mrs. Moss!

CAYLY. Oh. Hello. Finally, our newspaper delivery. Is the printing press up and running again?

COURIER. You betcha! *(Gives Cayly a newspaper.)* Here you are, Mrs. Moss. The not-so-daily-but-almost-weekly Kingdom Press newspaper! Hand delivered as promised.

CAYLY. Oh, thank you! We've been waiting for this one.

COURIER. Sorry for the delay, Miss. They could only do a short run printing of this edition last week, so I haven't been able to deliver to your region until today. Enjoy! Freshly printed! Freshly folded! And freshly scented!

CAYLY. Freshly scented?

COURIER. Indeed, Madam! A new thing the editors are trying out. Each section has its own scent.

CAYLY. How lovely!

COURIER. Yes! Quite lovely ... until you get to the obituaries. My advice. Skip that section.

CAYLY. I'll keep that in mind. Thank you!

COURIER. No problem, Miss. Thanks for being a not-so-daily-but-almost-weekly Kingdom Press subscriber! And have yourself a not-so-bad-but-almost-fantastic day! *(Exits out front door.)*

CAYLY. *(Looks over a few pages of the newspaper and*

sniffs.) Wow. Scented pages. *(Sniffs.)* The Baker's Lifestyle section smells delightful! *(Turns a page.)* The jousting tournament results. *(Sniffs.)* Not bad. *(Turns a page and sniffs again and then gags.)* Ugh ... what is that? Oh ... the obituaries ... oh my god! Blech! *(Turns another page.)* "Economy". *(Sniffs but then something on the page catches her eye.)* Oh. Wait. What's this? *(Reading.)* "King Amado's new decree one-one-seven ... temporarily raising taxes on all citizens ... for the good of the land ... no exceptions. Collections begin next week." Oh dear. *(Corbin Moss enters the front door; home after a busy day at work but unusually chipper.)*

CORBIN. Well, hello everyone!

OSWALDO. Hey, dad.

CORBIN. Oz, my boy! Mom is keeping you busy with your studies, I see. Those books look heavy. My father used to always say heavy books lead to heavy minds. And how is my wonderful wife this afternoon?

CAYLY. Well, Corbin, it's been an eventful day. Oz and I almost made it through each subject.

CORBIN. Oh good! *(Notices the book Oswaldo is reading.)* But hold on. You aren't making him read out of that "things to come" textbook again are you?

OSWALDO. She is.

CORBIN. Oh, come on, Cayly. The school system in this Kingdom is a subject of ridicule. The administrators should've never allowed The Future as a subject in their curriculum. And remember that the lessons taught by the King's subjects and even your own are not subject to their approval. So, you should do your own thing and not subject Oz to this ... subject.

OSWALDO. I agree!

CORBIN. Children shouldn't be forced to learn about things that may or may not even happen. The future isn't definite. And look ... *(Picks up Oswaldo's book.)* ... the authors of this book have dated all these events so far in the future that we'll be long gone before we find out if they actually happen or not. And it claims to have been written by the most enlightened soothsayers, the wisest sages, and the most mystical mystics in all the land. But what makes them so special if they can never prove their predictions? This book is nonsense.

CAYLY. I hear you, but as long as this book is in the curriculum our son is going to study it.

CORBIN. Well, maybe reading it won't hurt anything, but he should at least understand that it's all just make-believe. Fiction!

OSWALDO. But dad ...

CORBIN. I'm just sayin' read it. You don't have to believe it.

OSWALDO. A waste of time, but okay.

CORBIN. And now I want to share with you both some extraordinary news. You know how last week I talked about making an adjustment to my job title?

CAYLY. Yes. I remember you saying something about that.

CORBIN. You see, when I first started my business, I was just one of many Clock Fixer's in the kingdom. And business hasn't been necessarily bad, but we've always talked about how it could be better, right?

CAYLY. Yes. Of course.

CORBIN. Well, as of this week, I am no longer a 'Clock Fixer'. I am now the Kingdom's one and only 'Time Repair Specialist'.

CAYLY. Fancy change. I like it. Has it affected business?

CORBIN. Has it affected business? *(Reveals a hefty coin pouch and jingles it.)* You hear that? I would say that this proves it has. I get customers all day long. All of them wanting their "time repaired". And all of them wanting a "specialist" to do it. Just today, I was commissioned to fix three buzz watches, a door clock, a witching clock, a found under a rock clock, and two great uncle clocks. They were twins.

OSWALDO. Nice! I've never seen a witching clock in person! Are you still working on that one?

CORBIN. Sure am. You can join me at the workshop tomorrow if you like.

CAYLY. This is more money than you've ever made in a week.

CORBIN. I know. And the week isn't over yet!

CAYLY. Well, it's good timing.

CORBIN. *(Chuckles.)* I see what you did there.

CAYLY. No. I mean we're definitely going to need this now.

CORBIN. What do you mean? We're getting by fine already. We should be able to save all of the extra income.

CAYLY. *(Gives Corbin the Kingdom newspaper.)* You might want to take a look at the latest edition of the Not-so-daily-but-almost-weekly news.

CORBIN. Why? What's it say? *(Reading.)* "King Amado's new decree one-one-seven" …? New decree? Who does this new king think he is with all his "decrees? *(Reading.)* "… temporarily raising taxes …" Oh, great! Well, we know how long temporary is when it's in the King's language - Forever! *(Reading.)* "… for the good of the land …" The good of the land would be to get rid of this hack of a king. *(Reading.)* "... no exceptions. Collections begin next week." I can't believe it. For once, I take the initiative to better ourselves and it's going to amount to nothing because my extra earnings will be going to this new tax. And think about what this will do to the economy! My customer traffic will diminish for sure. Who's going to spend money to get their clocks fixed when they know there are new taxes to be paid!? Collections begin next week!?

CAYLY. Actually, there was a delay in the not-so-daily-but-almost-weekly Kingdom Press delivery. This article was released last week.

CORBIN. So, collections for this new tax start this week? Something must be done.

CAYLY. No one really knows much about our new king. When former King Azul passed away, his younger cousin Amado was the only living relative that remained, so he naturally took the throne.

CORBIN. Well, I naturally don't care. He was a distant relative at best and that's where he should stay – distant. They should have given the throne to someone else. You know who would've been a good King? That one knight with the missing arm that's always trying to give people back rubs. What's his name again?

CAYLY. Sir Jerry.

CORBIN. Sir Jerry! Nice guy right there. Nice guy. Friendly and kind. Did I mention sympathetic? Sympathetic enough not to be raising taxes on his citizens, I'm sure! *(Repeated knocking is heard at the door.)* I'm on my way if you just give me a second. *(As soon as Corbin answers the door, Henri enters. She's extremely nervous, impatient, out of breath, and constantly moving.)*

HENRI. Corbin! You're finally home! I need your help. I ran as quickly as I could down to your shop and when I got there, you know what I saw?

CORBIN. Henri, what? What did you see?!

HENRI. You were closed! You had already left for the day. So then I ran all the way here and you know what I saw when I arrived?

CORBIN. You saw that I was ... here?

HENRI. Yes! Help me, Corbin. Please!

CORBIN. Just calm down, Henri. What's going on?

HENRI. *(Reveals a watch from her pocket.)* My watch! It stopped almost two hours ago. My time is broken! Can you believe it? I've just lost two hours of my life. Two hours! Right now, I technically don't exist.

CORBIN. Henri. Just because your watch stopped … that doesn't mean your life stops.

HENRI. I'm dying here, Corbin! Repair me. Please!

CORBIN. Give me your watch. *(Henri gives him the watch. Corbin gets a small screwdriver or other small tool and begins working on it.)*

HENRI. Thank you, Corbin. Thank you! And please hurry. *(To Cayly.)* Hi, Cayly. I hope I'm not intruding.

CAYLY. Of course not. You're always welcome here. That's what neighbors are for.

HENRI. Oswaldo! I see you're busy with your studies. *(Notices Oswaldo's textbook.)* Oh my! You're studying the Future! What a wonderful subject! My favorite!

OSWALDO. Oh, really? Well, perhaps you can tell me why studying a future that's more than likely not going to happen is so important?

HENRI. What's more important than knowing what hasn't happened yet? It helps us to be ready. Ready for what's to come. I remember learning in school that the deceitful Clive Seamonger is going to one day sell phony credit coins and build an evil commercial empire from the profits. That's a good thing to know.

OSWALDO. Why?

HENRI. Because now I know not to buy credit coins from Clive Seamonger.

OSWALDO. Okay, but if we know in advance and decide not to buy the phony credit coins, doesn't that make this future I'm reading obsolete, therefore making it pointless to read?

CAYLY. Oz, please. Don't argue with Miss Hackus.

HENRI. The future is never obsolete. It's going to happen whether we like it or not.

OSWALDO. Yes, but what if the Seamonger family never even name one of their children Clive? I'm just saying there's no guarantee that it's going to happen the way it's stated in this book.

HENRI. I've never known a textbook to lie. They wouldn't be in schools if they lied.

OSWALDO. Well, I'm not in school, so maybe this one lies! *(Frustrated, he slams down the book and exits.)*

CAYLY. Oswaldo Mandias Moss! Do not throw your books around the house! And don't you slam that door! *(A door slams shut offstage.)* That child. I'm so sorry, Henry. He's been stressed lately.

HENRI. It's okay. So am I. Hmmm … I wonder … *(Picks up the same book and slams it down.)* Wow. You know, that really does help a little.

CORBIN. *(Gives Henri the watch.)* Okay. I got you all fixed up.

HENRI. Oh, thank you, Corbin. Thank you! How much do I owe you? You saved my life!

CORBIN. Don't worry about it. You're a friend.

HENRI. I must.

CAYLY. No, really. We can't take your money.

HENRI. I can't believe that I have friends like you. And I know those two hours are lost forever and I'll never get them back, but I just want you to know, if I still had those hours, I would share them with you, buddy. *(Another knock at the door.)*

CAYLY. Who could it be now? *(She opens the door, revealing Richard Taxman with his tax-collecting satchel.)*

TAXMAN. Greetings, good citizens!

CAYLY. *(Nervously.)* Oh, hello, Taxman. Can we help you?

TAXMAN. *(Enters their home; like a boss.)* I have been sent to this region by King Amado himself to collect the monthly taxes as well as the new tax initiated in decree one-one-seven. Please do not hesitate to offer me tea or biscuits for I have been in the presence of his majesty.

CORBIN. Oh, I don't think so, Mr. Taxman. You can tell the King that the Moss family will only be paying their normal monthly dues and his new decree belongs in the trash.

TAXMAN. What? You dare speak of King Amado's policies in that manner? Plus, you refuse me hospitality?

HENRI. Corbin! What're you doing? We all must pay the new tax.

CORBIN. I'm telling you that I'm not paying this decree one-one whatever. *(Gives Taxman a small pouch of money.)* Here. This is the regular monthly dues.

TAXMAN. You silly man. You cannot ignore decree one-one-seven. Do you not know that it is for the good of the land?

CORBIN. Blah, blah, good of the land, no exceptions. I got all that.

CAYLY. Maybe we should just pay it.

CORBIN. Absolutely not! I refuse.

TAXMAN. You can't refuse. I refuse to let you refuse.

CORBIN. Well, maybe you should take your little purse and refuse yourself out of our house.

TAXMAN. I refuse to let you talk to me this way. And how dare you insult the royal tax-collecting satchel!

HENRI *(Gives Taxman a small coin pouch.)* Here, Mr. Taxman. I'll pay it. Take this. No need for all this refusing.

This should cover the new tax for my friends.

CORBIN. What're you doing? Give me that! *(Takes the coin pouch from Taxman.)* I'm not paying it and I'm not going to let you pay it for me.

HENRI. I owe you for repairing my watch.

TAXMAN. I'll take that coin pouch. Thank you. *(He takes the pouch from Corbin.)* And now, I shall be on my -

CORBIN. Oh no you don't! *(Takes the coin pouch back.)*

TAXMAN. Hey! Give me that back!

CORBIN. Henry. That's not the point. The point is that I don't want this new young hack of a King to feel like he can just create new taxes whenever he feels like it.

TAXMAN. You call King Amado a hack?! I refuse to hear this! You, sir, are not worthy to live in this kingdom.

HENRI. No, sir, Mr. Taxman, sir. He really is worthy. Here's the payment back! *(Takes the coin pouch from Corbin and hands it to Taxman.)*

CORBIN. Henri! Stop it. *(Takes the coin pouch back from Taxman.)*

HENRI. Corbin, I can't let you do this.

CORBIN. Yes you can. And you will.

HENRI. Just give him the coins.

CORBIN. No way!

TAXMAN. I refuse to put up with this, gentlemen.

HENRI. Just continue to refuse a little while longer and we'll get back to you in a second, sir. *(Aside to Corbin and Cayly.)* Hey, do you remember that Dobson fellow that lived over on the Nightingale path?

CAYLY. You talking about tall Dobson or short Dobson?

HENRI. Short Dobson.

CORBIN. Yeah, so what?

HENRI. Well, I heard from Shawn Meadowmaker that the

reason Dobson isn't living there anymore is because he didn't pay his Kingdom dues. No one has seen him in a few weeks. They say that he's locked up in the castle dungeon where every day he's tortured. And sometimes when the guards want a little more entertainment, they feed one of his fingers to the royal lions!

CORBIN. Look. I'm paying what is owed. I'm just not giving one cent to this new tax. Get it?

HENRI. In the tax man world, it's all or nothing. Pay it all, or I fear they'll do something drastic to you. Please Corbin!

CAYLY. Henri's right. I don't want anything happening to you or Oz.

CORBIN. Nothing is going to happen. And that's the end of it. *(To Taxman.)* Here, Taxman. Take what I originally gave you, and nothing more. Those are the terms.

TAXMAN. Very well, sir. You will find that your refusal was not a wise decision. King Amado shall hear of this! And you will rule the day that you refused me!!

CORBIN. *(Awkward pause.)* Are you trying to say "rue the day"?

TAXMAN. That's what I said. You will rule the day, you filthy swines! Now be gone!

CORBIN. This is our house.

TAXMAN. Fine! *(He exits out the front door.)*

HENRY. Corbin! What have you done?!

CORBIN. Well, you heard him. I rule today! And I made a stand. I did exactly what I said I was going to do. And it feels great!

HENRY. It won't feel great when they put you in the torture chamber. Or hang you out on the gallows. Or start feeding your fingers to the royal lions!

CAYLY. Now, hold on! I get a say in this too. Corbin, go back out there and give him the rest of what we owe.

CORBIN. There's not gonna be any torture. At least ... I hope not.

CAYLY. Well, what're we gonna do if the retaliation for this is severe?

HENRI. Yes, what're we gonna do!?

CORBIN. I have a plan, okay. And I need you, Henry.

HENRI. Anything! I'm here for you.

CORBIN. We're going to dethrone King Amado.

CAYLY. What?!

HENRI. By "anything", I mean all things but that.

CORBIN. Just hear me out.

CAYLY. You know that plotting to overthrow the King is treason, don't you?

HENRI. Treason?! I'm outta here! *(Heads for the front door.)* Thanks for fixing my watch! See you guys later. Maybe.

CORBIN. Henri, wait! *(Henri stops.)* Remember? You owe me.

HENRI. What?

CORBIN. Two hours. You owe me two hours of your time. I'm asking for those two hours right now. Stay.

HENRI. Stay? I suppose I could stay a little while longer. It was actually only one hour and forty-seven minutes though, not a full two hours.

CORBIN. Just stay and help me for the next hour and forty-seven minutes and then you can leave.

HENRI. What're you gonna have me do?

CORBIN. This King Amado is new, right? There can't be that many people that support him. So technically, I'm thinking we already have the advantage. And his demand for the citizens to give him more of their hard-earned money from their pockets might be a useful tool for pulling other people in our favor. What we need to do is recruit others. We need a team.

CAYLY. Well, that would certainly take the focus off just you, if you had others to support you. Who do you have in mind?

HENRI. Oh, I don't like this. I don't like this one bit. It's too risky.

CORBIN. Just help me think for a moment.

HENRI. Better be quick. There's no telling when the guards will be here to take you away.

CAYLY. So far, we have three. Me, you, and Henri.

HENRI. I'm only temporary.

CAYLY. Let's figure out what other strengths we need to fill in the gaps. How about we start writing down a list? *(Grabs a quill and paper and prepares to start writing names.)*

CORBIN. Yes. Good idea. To start, I think we need someone who is familiar with all the laws of the land. And I mean every law, every decree, everything. There may be a way to put King Amado out of power with little effort. Maybe he's already broken a legacy law or something that can remove him.

CAYLY. You're right! Something like that happened to Baron Salamander in Floridia years ago. And there have been so many laws passed over the years that a lot of them have been forgotten. I bet if we found someone who was an expert with the laws, we might be able to find a loophole that could end King Amado's reign.

HENRI. D. Duncan.

CORBIN. But who in the land is that knowledgeable with the laws? This is going to be tough.

HENRI. D. Duncan.

CAYLY. Oh, Willy Shoeman! He used to study a lot.

CORBIN. He went a bit mad though, right? Last I heard, he was paranoid an elf was trying to steal his Brandy.

HENRI. D. Duncan.

CAYLY. Well, that guy should be staying clear of alcohol anyway.

CORBIN. Brandy was his wife.

HENRI. D. Duncan! D. Duncan is the man you want.

CAYLY. Why are you stuttering?

HENRI. I'm not. First initial D. Last name Duncan. D. Duncan. D is the best. He knows everything. If there's a loophole, the D. can surely find it.

CORBIN. D. Duncan, eh? Okay. We'll give this Duncan law man a shot. Good work, Henri. See. Doesn't it feel good to help?

HENRI. Maybe a little.

CAYLY. Okay, next I think we need a good speaker and motivator.

CORBIN. Yes. Someone who has outstanding language skills and can persuade people to join our side. *(To Henri.)* Anyone coming to mind, Henri?

HENRI. Hmmm ... the most persuasive speaker I've ever known is Deke Harvey. He's very efficient with spoken words.

CORBIN. Is he a professional motivator or something?

HENRI. Insurance salesman.

CORBIN. Just how good with words is he?

HENRI. Not long ago, he talked me into buying dragon fire insurance. Anything damaged by dragon's fire is covered under my policy.

CORBIN. *(Confused.)* Henri. Dragons don't exist.

HENRI. I know.

CORBIN. Point taken.

CAYLY. I'll add him to the list.

CORBIN. Now, on that same line of thought, it would also be beneficial to get someone who's good with written words.

HENRI. You going to write the King a letter?

CORBIN. No, not to the King. We need someone that can reach the public - the citizens of the land. Someone that can influence with their written words. Deke may be a good speaker, but printed material can reach a wider crowd. Oh wait! Hand me the Kingdom Press, Cayly.

CAYLY. Here you go. *(She gives Corbin the newspaper.)*

CORBIN. *(Gagging at the smell.)* What is that?! Smells like a sour rotting corpse!!

CAYLY. Oh. Sorry. Accidentally, gave you the obituaries section. Here's the article. *(She gives him the Economy section.)*

CORBIN. Estelle Avery. She's the one that wrote this article about the new decree. It couldn't hurt to find out her true opinion on the matter. Plus, if she sympathizes with us, her written words would reach everyone in the Kingdom, and could gain us more support.

HENRI. Estelle Avery!

CAYLY. You a fan?

HENRI. She's wonderful! I loved her article last month on overcrowded schools leading to undercrowded young minds. Very insightful!

CORBIN. Okay, that's a good start for our revolution. Henri, you go and find D. Duncan. Cayly, you contact the newspaper and see if you can reach Estelle. And I'll go see if Deke Harvey is currently in his office.

HENRI. Okay. I'll do it.

CORBIN. Alright. It's time to gather our team. You both know who you're in charge of gathering. I gather this may not be an easy task, but gathering a team never is. Gather them up and then we'll all gather back here. Once we all return, we'll have a ... a ... gathering.

End of scene.

ACT ONE
Scene 2

Later that afternoon. The throne room of King Amado. The room is decorated in royal blue décor - throne with royal blue cushions, royal blue curtains, etc. A canvas sits on an easel facing upstage so that the audience can't see what is painted on it.

At rise, Leon, wearing the King's crown and royal blue robe, is standing alone in the room – (this is meant for the audience to mistake him for an insane king).

LEON. *(Looking around maniacally.)* What's that noise? I hear it. It's creeping around like a shadow at the noon. I hear you, shadow. My enemy. I hear the sweet serenade sung from your murky lips. You shall give me immortality, shadow, for I am your King! Follow me and you shall prosper. Disobey me and you will become fond of my cold icy grip just like the peasants. *(Listens.)* What's that you say? You choose to follow a more worthy King? Well, let me tell you this, shadow. It is you that isn't worthy of my presence. Leave my throne room! Leave at once! Go live with the commoners for you shall not find a more worthy King. *(He takes off his crown and insanely stares at it.)* Ah! The crown. My crown. My mistress. My love. I am nothing without you, yet I am everything. Everything this kingdom needs. Everything you need. You're nothing without me, for I am everything. *(His mood suddenly changes.)* Oh no, what is this? Please, crown, my love. Don't cry. *(He starts to pet the crown.)* There, there. While it's true that you are indeed nothing without me, I promise you, my love, my mistress, my sweet angel, I shall not leave you. And you shall not leave me, for I will not allow it. *(He hears something.)* Did you hear that, my love? He's back. Is that you? Shadow, are you still here? This shall not take long, my dear. *(Places the crown on the throne, and then turns and listens.)* I can hear you breathing, shadow. I take your return as a sign of loyalty, but what if it's too late. What if I tell you that your presence is no longer welcome here? *(Listening.)* Mercy? You speak of mercy? You long for the King to show you mercy? *(Bold maniacal laugher.)* I have mercy for you, shadow. And I have given it a name. *(He unsheathes a dagger.)* Its name is death! *(He begins violently stabbing the ground.)* Feel the deep would of my dagger! Here is your mercy! Doesn't mercy feel delightful, shadow! Does it?!?! *(He slowly stops stabbing as he realizes that his shadow meant the world to him.)* What have you done, shadow? No. What have I done? You could have had everything. We could have reigned together. *(He drops his dagger.)* Lifeless. I will never forget you. I shall rain a thousand deaths on the land to compensate for your departure. You shall be memorialized. *(He returns to the crown. King Amado enters behind him and watches for a moment, unnoticed by Leon.)* I'm so terribly sorry you had to witness that, my love. My actions are inexcusable yet justified. Please forgive me.

AMADO. Well, I must know what you've done before I can issue forgiveness.

LEON. *(Startled.)* Oh! King Amado! Your majesty.

AMADO. It's majesty now? What happened to your "love"? Why were you just stabbing my floor with your dagger? And what're wearing, Leon? This doesn't look like your normal jester clothes. Wait, is that my robe?

LEON. *(Nervous.)* It's a ... costume? Yes! I was just ... umm ... rehearsing a theatrical piece I've written.

AMADO. *(Regarding the crown.)* Did you touch this?

LEON. Your crown? Um ... define touch.

AMADO. It doesn't matter. I have an assignment for you.

LEON. Yes, your majesty?

AMADO. *(Reveals a sealed envelope with the royal blue seal.)* Take this letter across the river to Werner. Give it to the project manager. Make sure everything is going as planned. If something doesn't look right according to the designs I showed you, let me know immediately.

LEON. Sure thing, your majesty.

AMADO. And remember, the project is to remain a secret for now. Is that clear?

LEON. Of course.

AMADO. Good. Now go. But first, tell me a joke.

LEON. A joke?

AMADO. Yes. Any joke. You're a jester. Say something funny.

LEON. How bout I do a little dance instead? *(Begins doing a terribly silly dance.)*

AMADO. No dancing. I said a joke.

LEON. Okay. A joke. Well, let's see …

AMADO. Actually, I have a joke to tell you instead.

LEON. You tell jokes, sir?

AMADO. Why not? You are my JEST-er and people call me ma-JEST-y, so we should both be allowed to do some JEST-ing, amiright?

LEON. I suppose so.

AMADO. See what I did there? *(Beat.)* That was the joke. My JEST-er? Ma-JEST-y? JEST-ing? *(Shrugs him off.)* Ah, you don't know humor. Go do something important before

I have your arms chopped off.

LEON. I'm sorry, sire?

AMADO. Another joke, Leon! Come on. You're killing me here. *(Taxman enters carrying his satchel.)*

TAXMAN. Pardon me, sire, but we have a problem in the Sharlay region.

AMADO. Well, if it isn't Richard Taxman. How does the tax collecting go?

TAXMAN. There is a certain individual who lives in a certain little quaint house with his certain inhospitable family on the corner of Parker and Zoe that certainly refuses to pay the decree one-one-seven tax.

AMADO. Are you certain?

TAXMAN. Certainly!

AMADO. He refuses?

TAXMAN. He refuses, your majesty!

AMADO. Did you tell him it was for the good of the land?

TAXMAN. I tell him it was for the good of the land!

AMADO. And he still refuses?

TAXMAN. He still refuses! I have never seen the likes of this kind of refusing in all my lives!

AMADO. Who is this certain individual?

TAXMAN. His name is Corbin Moss, sire.

LEON. Corbin? Oh yeah, he's the new Time Repair Specialist in town. I hear he's the best.

AMADO. A Time Repair Specialist? Wow. That sounds important. How many Time Repair Specialists are there in the Kingdom?

LEON. He's the one and only. A member of the royal trumpeter squad told me that Corbin fixed his buzz watch in record time.

AMADO. Surely you jest.

LEON. I do. Sometimes. But not about this.

TAXMAN. This man monopolizes the time repairing industry. He's obviously profiting from his business and still refuses to pay the tax.

AMADO. Interesting. Make your rounds across the next region in your route. On your way back, visit Mr. Moss again. Tell him that the palace has decided to extend him another opportunity to pay the new decree tax.

TAXMAN. But, your majesty, the deadline has passed for the Sharlay region. And Corbin has missed it. We cannot extend his deadline.

AMADO. Who says?

TAXMAN. The King, of course!

AMADO. And who's the King?

TAXMAN. *(It sinks in.)* Right … well, what I mean to say is that, in the past, the palace has never extended tax deadlines.

AMADO. The history books may show that the standard monthly taxes are never extended, but what do they say about the new decree one-one-seven tax?

TAXMAN. Well … nothing that I'm aware of, your majesty.

AMADO. And has any sage or mystic ever said anything about decree one-one-seven when they foretold the future?

TAXMAN. Not to my knowledge.

AMADO. So, what's stopping me from extending the deadline?

TAXMAN. Nothing, I suppose, but...

AMADO. Then I suppose you should stop by and make another request for the tax.

TAXMAN. And if he refuses again?

AMADO. If he refuses again, then it will be known that you, Richard Taxman, are not a very good tax man.

TAXMAN. What?! I am the best! Collecting taxes has been an occupation in my family for generations.

AMADO. Then show them what you're made of! There's a tax to be collected and you must collect it.

TAXMAN. But this Corbin fellow didn't even offer me tea when I visited him.

AMADO. There's no time for tea when there are taxes to collect.

TAXMAN. And he called you a hack.

AMADO. What does that even mean?

TAXMAN. I'm not quite sure.

AMADO. Then why do I care? Go Taxman. Go and be the best tax man that you can be. Leon here was just telling me that he has always wanted to try a little tax collecting himself. I may have to give him a shot if you fail.

TAXMAN. What?! Him?!

LEON. Actually, I don't quite remember saying that.

AMADO. Yes! Him! His cousin is a tax man over in Werner and he has been showing Leon the ropes. *(To Leon with a wink.)* Isn't that right, Leon?

LEON. Ummm … well …

AMADO. See! He's going to be a great tax man in no time.

TAXMAN. This man. This fool. A tax man? *(Laughs.)* Look at his hands. These are the hands of a simpleton. Coins, bills, and IOU's do not belong in these hands. *(To Leon.)* You! Jester! Look at me! *(Leon does.)* Now look over there! *(Leon does.)* Now look at the floor! *(Leon does.)* Turn around! *(Leon does and Taxman yells.)* Ah!

LEON. *(Startled.)* Ah!

TAXMAN. Who's that behind you?!

LEON. Uhh ... no one is behind me.

TAXMAN. Of course not, because now they're in front of

you with a dagger to your throat!

AMADO. *(Playing along.)* No! Leon! Get out of there! He's got a knife!

LEON. What is happening right now!?

TAXMAN. You're dead! That's what happened. Just as I thought. Look at the motion in his neck. How are you ever supposed to keep a lookout behind you with neck motion like this? Tax collecting is a dangerous business, you know. You're all alone out there. Vulnerable. You collect from the wrong person on the wrong day and it's ... *(Makes a cut throat dying noise.)* Window shades.

LEON. Window shades?

TAXMAN. Dead! Here, hold this. *(He gives Leon the satchel and he can't help but hold it awkwardly. Taxman laughs.)* You have the strength of a hairless cat. There's no way you could carry your collections across each region. You do not belong in the tax collecting world!

AMADO. Go then, Taxman! Show the kingdom you mean business.

TAXMAN. *(Proudly.)* Do you see this satchel? This satchel belonged to the cousin of my great great great grandfather on my mother's side and I have inherited his legacy. You shall have your tax, sire. I will see to it! *(He exits.)*

AMADO. That was ... a purse, right? I saw that, right? A lady's purse?

LEON. It looked that way to me too, your majesty.

AMADO. Well, okay then. Leon?

LEON. Yes?

AMADO. The letter I gave you. Take it to Werner. Go.

LEON. Oh right! I'm on it.

AMADO. Leon?

LEON. Yes?

AMADO. Don't forget your dagger.

LEON. Oh right! *(Picks up dagger from the ground.)* I've been wondering where that's been.

AMADO. And Leon?

LEON. Yes, your majesty?

AMADO. Never touch my crown again.

LEON. Of course. Never again, sire.

AMADO. Off you go. *(Leon exits.)*

    End of scene.

ACT ONE
Scene 3

Back in the Moss residence.

At rise, Cayly is frantically cleaning up, making sure everything looks nice for the guests soon to arrive. Corbin enters with Deke Harvey, a nicely dressed, smooth talking salesman carrying a briefcase.

DEKE. ... and so I told her, ya know, with the right tools, there really is more than one way to skin a cat.

CORBIN. *(Laughs.)* You missed out on a career as a comedian, Mr. Harvey. My side hurts! You could sell your jokes for top dollar!

DEKE. Already am. Expect a bill in the mail. *(Corbin laughs and then stops as he realizes Deke may be serious.)*

CORBIN. Cayly! Were you able to contact Estelle?

CAYLY. Yes.

CORBIN. And?

CAYLY. She said she'd like to hear more about your plan. And when I told her that I was homeschooling Oz, she wanted to come by immediately to interview him for a follow up to her undercrowded minds story. She's here right now talking to him.

CORBIN. That's fantastic! Cayly, this is Mr. Deke Harvey.

DEKE. Very nice to meet you. And please, no need for formalities. The name is Deke.

CAYLY. Great to meet you, Deke.

CORBIN. Alright. Henry will be arriving soon with the law expert.

DEKE. *(Reveals a folder from his briefcase.)* While we wait, I'd like you to have a look at my full portfolio of insurance policies available. Let me know what suits you. I mean, a suit's only worth wearing if you've got matching shoes, right?

CORBIN. What? No. Actually we don't really need any of that.

DEKE. You could've fooled me. Look at this place.

CAYLY. What about it?

DEKE. Flammable is what it is. I'm surprised this place is still standing. Really. Look at all these watches and clocks. Fire magnets I call 'em. They got a mind of their own. Always ticking like that. Tik-tok, tik-tok, tik-tok. They're counting down to something, I tell ya. Do you really want to wait and see what that something is? And don't even get me started on how moody a grandfather clock can be. So, how bout it? I can get you signed up for a clock fire insurance policy right here today. No - come to think of it, let's get you flame insurance instead.

CAYLY. Yes, I think that would work well for us. We do have a lot of watches coming in and out of here often. Corbin is always bringing his work home with him.

CORBIN. No, Cayly. We don't need any of that. *(Beat.)* Wait. There's a difference between fire and flame insurance?

DEKE. It's all in the color, my friend. All in the color.

CORBIN. Sorry, but insurance is not a priority right now.

DEKE. Look at you. Taking control. I like that. Let me introduce another proposition. Me and you. We're both business people, am I right?

CORBIN. I'd say so.

DEKE. Then let's talk business. Let me ask you something. You fix up all these watches?

CORBIN. *(Proudly.)* Yes. I'm a Time Repair Specialist

DEKE. Nice and elegant. Ok, Mr. Moss, I'd like to make a deal. I'll help you with your plan to get rid of our foul King and in exchange, whenever you fix up a watch, you do a bit of cross selling and direct your customers to me for some watch insurance.

CORBIN. That's actually not a horrible idea.

DEKE. I'll even leave you some flyers that you can hang in your shop to promote the insurance. It'll have a picture of an exploding watch on it. And it will say "Contact Deke Harvey today for your explosion insurance".

CORBIN. Watches don't generally explode.

DEKE. Right! I get it. Careful communication. My mistake. "Contact Deke Harvey today for your rapid disassembly insurance".

CORBIN. You'll have to cover more than just explosions or... rapid disassembly. I think it should say that any future damages of any kind will be covered.

DEKE. Past? Present? Future? Time is irrelevant when everywhere you go all you see are dogs going hungry in the streets.

CAYLY. He's got a point.

CORBIN. I don't even know what that means. How bout just make sure those flyers say any damages covered and we have a deal. I don't want to be in the business of scamming my clients.

DEKE. The true negotiator. You have yourself a deal. *(Attempts to shake hands.)* Put 'er there? And your cut will be two per cent.

CORBIN. *(Extends his hand but quickly pulls it back.)*

Wait. That doesn't sound standard. Surely six to eight per cent would be more reasonable?

DEKE. Naturally, but if you're only wearing one glove, how do you plan on keeping both your hands warm? Come on, put 'er there. *(Hand still extended.)*

CORBIN. *(Hesitates and then shakes Deke's hand.)* I guess that sounds ... wait! Hey, you are good. Henry was right. How do you do that? *(Henri enters the front door with Duncan, the local law librarian. Duncan is carrying a huge law book.)*

HENRI. Okay, Corbin. I did what you said. It wasn't easy since he's a bit of a local celebrity, but this here is *the* D. Duncan. Librarian of the Sharlay Law Offices and I can vouch that D. is the best in town. He knows every law, every decree. This team needs D. There's no way we can do this without the D. Coming up with a plan is going to get tense, and D. will be there for us in those situations. We can all benefit from having D. in our lives.

DUNCAN. Please. Just call me Duncan.

CAYLY. Oh? You know, my aunt Francis used to like to go by her last name as well.

DUNCAN. Duncan is my first name.

CORBIN. Your name is Duncan Duncan?

DUNCAN. Family tradition.

HENRI. He comes from a long line of D's.

CORBIN. Right. So, I'm assuming that Henry has told you about our plan?

DUNCAN. You want to remove King Amado from the throne and do away with this new tax?

CORBIN. Exactly.

HENRI. *(Notices Deke.)* Woah. Deke Harvey! Good to see you, buddy!

DEKE. Oh, Heeey ... *(Can't remember his name.)* ...

youuuuu!

HENRI. Henri.

DEKE. Henri! Of course. How are the kids?

HENRI. I don't have any kids...

DEKE. *(His best fake laugh.)* Of course not. I just mean in general. You know, 'How are the kids? ... everywhere ..."

HENRI. They're all good ... I guess.

CORBIN. Henri was telling us how you sold him dragon fire insurance a few months ago.

DEKE. In very high demand this season. You got a package deal with that, correct?

HENRI. Yes, siree. I'm very pleased.

CORBIN. Package deal? What else was included?

HENRI. He sold me the color blue.

CORBIN. A blue what?

HENRI. The entire color blue. It's mine. I own it.

DEKE. That was a steal, I might add.

CORBIN. Clearly. *(Estelle enters from the hallway. She is a quick-witted journalist for the Kingdom Press.)*

ESTELLE. Such a smart boy you have there, Mrs. Moss.

CAYLY. Well, I don't really have any teaching experience but I'm doing my best.

ESTELLE. I'm impressed. You're really making him think outside of the box. Doing away with The Future textbook is such a bold move. How do you think the authors would feel if they knew of your nontraditional teaching techniques?

CAYLY. Did Oz say that we were getting rid of that subject?

ESTELLE. It's bloody brilliant!

CAYLY. Thanks!

CORBIN. Estelle Avery. I'm Corbin. Cayly's husband.

ESTELLE. Corbin. I want you to know that I'm with you one hundred per cent. I miss our old King. King Azul was a kind and noble leader. And this new guy has been staying low. He must be aware that the people don't agree with his policies. Either that or he's hideous.

CORBIN. Thank you all for coming. I'd like to begin by having a discussion of what actions we can take to succeed in removing our new King from power.

DEKE. The floor is yours. What do you need us to do?

CORBIN. First, we need to figure out all of the possible scenarios in which a King can be dethroned. We have Duncan here who is going to fill us in on the technicalities.

DUNCAN. I have your answer, sir. Memorized. No need to even look it up.

CORBIN. Okay. Tell us.

DUNCAN. Just give me one second. I should look it up so that I don't misstate any of the details. *(Flips through pages of his law book.)* Ah. Here it is. *(Reading.)* "A King can only be removed from power if he or it becomes deceased, as in no life remaining in their bodies, as in their soul being removed from their bones, as in breathing is no longer an involuntary or voluntary action, nor is it an option. Manner of death does not matter for being deceased is not a temporary status. Once it is announced that the King has become deceased and has been removed from power in this way, which is the only way, there is naturally no way for that King to ever regain it. An heir must be available to take their place within forty-eight hours. If no heir is found within forty-eight hours, a woodland creature shall act as interim King until a suitable replacement is found."

CAYLY. Well, surely there must be another way. I mean ... we can't kill him. Can we?

CORBIN. Of course, we aren't going to kill him.

HENRI. Oh, good. I've never killed anyone before. I can't

imagine I'd be very good at it. What with the screaming and all.

ESTELLE. Just do it quickly, so they don't have time to scream.

HENRI. No. I mean, I'd be the one doing all the screaming.

CORBIN. Wait, Duncan. What was that last bit?

DUNCAN. The part about the woodland creature?

CORBIN. Not that. There was a bit about there being no way for the King to regain it if he loses it.

DUNCAN. *(Reading.)* "Once it is announced that the King has been removed from power in this way, which is the only way, there is -"

CORBIN. That's it. We can work with that.

DEKE. What are you cookin' up, Corbin?

CORBIN. Once it is "announced" that the King is dead, he can never regain the throne.

ESTELLE. Okay, but that still involves murdering him, right?

CORBIN. Only slightly.

CAYLY. What does that mean?

CORBIN. All we have to do is stage his death. It doesn't have to really happen.

HENRI. It doesn't?

CORBIN. Not at all. Tell me something, Estelle. How long would it take you to get an article out to the public announcing the King's death?

ESTELLE. If I stamp it as breaking news, I can get a statement to our printers in no time.

CORBIN. Okay, so if we can make it look like the King is dead, if only for a moment ...

ESTELLE. And then you want me to write an article announcing he's dead ...

DEKE. And once announced, the King can never regain power.

CAYLY. It's brilliant!

HENRI. But how do we make it look like the King is dead? We'd need some type of proof. She can't just publish an article with no proof.

CORBIN. I don't know. But we can think this through.

ESTELLE. Staging something common would be more believable.

DEKE. Well, what's the most common cause of death around here?

CORBIN. I don't have statistics like that. It'll take some research.

DUNCAN. I have that information, sir. *(Flips through pages in his law book.)* Ah, here it is. Statistics. *(Browsing.)* Death ... death ... death ... ah, here we go. The number one cause of death in the land is "fishing".

CORBIN. Fishing? What does that mean? Are there really that many fishing accidents to make it the number one cause of death?

DUNCAN. It all has to do with the Aquatic Citizens Act in the fifty-third decree. It states that all fish in Kingdom waters are deemed citizens of the land, so therefore every time a fish is caught, the Kingdom has one less citizen. Of course, no one has ever been arrested for fish murders. The fish citizens are way behind on paying their taxes, so they get very limited government protection.

HENRI. Oh no. I'm a lowdown filthy murderer.

CORBIN. That's simply ridiculous. Okay, what does the book say is the next most common cause of death?

DUNCAN. Cannibalism. *(A beat as everyone stares confusingly at Duncan.)* It's another fish thing.

CORBIN. Is there anything in there that doesn't pertain to

fish or fishing or anything aquatic?

DUNCAN. How about death by poison?

CAYLY. Poison?

CORBIN. Hmm ... let's think of something else.

DEKE. Hold it. Let's visit this poison option for a moment. I know a guy, who knows a widow, who knows another guy that used to be good friends with an amateur alchemist, who knows how to create a formula that when drank will make you appear dead for twenty-four hours.

HENRI. Does it really work?

DEKE. More or less. It's in pill form and needs about 10 seconds to dissolve in a drink.

CORBIN. So, if we can get this stuff and somehow get the King to drink it, he will appear dead?

DEKE. For twenty-four hours. And the guy owes me, so I can get it cheap.

CORBIN. Okay. That might be the best idea we have for now, so let's work with that.

CAYLY. But how do we get King Amado to drink it?

ESTELLE. Leave that to me. I have a publicist pass. I can tell them that I'm in need of an urgent story and I want to do a piece on the King's wine collection or something like that. Surely, he'll offer me a sample. And I'll just refuse to drink, unless he joins me. I can slip it in his glass when he's distracted.

CORBIN. That's good! The King does have his own winery so that's not a bad idea at all! It's great. Believable. Perfect. But it's also very bold of you, Ms. Avery. It'll be risky to attempt poisoning his drink while in the palace.

DEKE. Just remember it takes 10 seconds to dissolve.

HENRI. Excuse me. I agree that this is a huge risk and before we go any further with this plan, I'd like to present the option of visiting a sage before we take on this mission.

CORBIN. Why would we want to do that?

HENRI. Because a sage will know if this plan is going to work. We would save ourselves a lot of trouble if we already knew ahead of time if this plan was going to succeed or not.

CORBIN. Henri, listen to what you're saying.

DUNCAN. Are we really going to visit a sage? I've never met a real sage before. This is tremendously exciting.

CORBIN. No, we're not gonna visit a sage.

HENRI. Well, I don't think I can be a part of this unless we visit a wise sage first.

CAYLY. *(Aside to Corbin.)* Just take them to a sage. What could it hurt?

CORBIN. Okay, Henri. Fine. But find one that lives close by, so that we can get moving with the plan. *(To Deke.)* Deke, you work on getting that pill while we're gone and bring it to Estelle. *(Knocking is heard at the front door.)*

TAXMAN. *(Outside door.)* Alright, scoundrels! I have returned by request of his royal majesty. He has compassion and is willing to give you another chance at paying your decree one-one-seven tax. Do not hesitate to invite me into your home and cook me a fine dinner for I have been in the presence of his majesty. Roasted duck is preferred, but smoked salmon with a side of toasted baguettes would be acceptable.

CORBIN. *(He opens the front door.)* I've already told you that we're not paying this new tax.

TAXMAN. *(Peeking in and seeing the group.)* What is going on here? I hope you're all here to talk some sense into this foolish man.

CORBIN. Actually, they would like to be reimbursed for paying this new tax. *(He takes Taxman's satchel.)*

TAXMAN. Hey! How dare you touch my satchel! Give it

back!

CORBIN. Here everyone. If you've already paid, then reach into this purse and take your portion back, and not a coin more. *(Deke, Duncan, Henri, and Estelle all dig through the satchel and take coins.)*

TAXMAN. This is outrageous! Get your disgraceful grubby fingers off my satchel! King Amado will hear of this!

CORBIN. Are you sure about that?

TAXMAN. Are you threatening me? I refuse to hear this.

CORBIN. No threats. But do you really want King Amado to know that you were just robbed by a couple of commoners? And that someone besides you touched the royal tax collecting purse?

TAXMAN. You will not get away with this, I tell you. I do not feel sorry for the punishment coming your way.

CORBIN. Deke. Do your thing.

DEKE. Taxman was it? All this talk of punishment has got my gears turning. Now, I'm no pie baker, but it looks to me like you could use a bit of wind insurance for your travels, my friend.

TAXMAN. Wind insurance?

DEKE. Oh yeah! All the collectors in the Kingdom have been signing up. Let's say you're walking along, doing your duty, collecting for the month. All of a sudden, a gust of wind pushes along your path and scoops you up. I mean, a breeze might be like a handshake, but all handshakes have an evil side, am I right?

TAXMAN. Oh dear …

DEKE. Now, let me ask you this. Where does this gust of wind take you? Where does it take you?

TAXMAN. *(A bit terrified.)* Well, I don't know.

DEKE. Exactly! No one knows. Now take a look in my portfolio where all of the different options are illustrated in bar graphs, line graphs, and hot apple pie graphs.

CORBIN. *(Aside to Cayly.)* While he's occupied we're going to slip out of here. Duncan, Henri, and I will go to the sage. You stay here with Estelle and get a game plan together for when she goes to the palace. We should be back soon. *(While Deke is chatting with Taxman- Corbin, Henri, and Duncan ease out the front door.)*

DEKE. I'm tellin' you, wind is public enemy number one, Taxman. It blows. It burns. It shifts and turns. You ever notice how it moves about like a stealthy assassin? It's hunting. It's a predator looking for prey. And that prey ... is you! *(Taxman's eyes get wide with fear.)*

 End of scene.

ACT ONE
Scene 4

Back in the palace.

At rise, King Amado is looking at a canvas that's on an easel. The canvas is facing upstage so that the audience can't see what is on it. Two royal guards, Bellywax and Herman, are standing across the room.

AMADO. *(To the Guards.)* You there.

HERMAN. *(Pointing to Bellywax.)* Are you referring to 'im, sir?

BELLYWAX. No. He was clearly talking to you. Didn't you hear the way he said "you" and "there". The inflection in his voice on the word "there" was an obvious indication that he was referring to the spot you are currently standing in.

HERMAN. I 'eard no reflection in 'is voice.

BELLYWAX. All you ever want to do is argue.

AMADO. Both of you. Come here and look at this new design.

HERMAN. Are you referring to us, sir?

BELLYWAX. Forgive my colleague's outrageous behaviour, sir.

HERMAN. 'ey! I 'ave no raging be'aviour! I'm quite civilized.

AMADO. Both of you! Shut up! Now, look at this canvas

and tell me what you think.

BELLYWAX. Sure thing! *(The Guards walk over and both take a moment to look at the canvas in admiration.)*

HERMAN. It's nice. I like the greenish green in the pattern there. I 'ave seen that type of green before. I have. I mean, it's got green qualities, but it also 'as this wavy shade of green in it. What kind of green do you call that, sir?

AMADO. It's ... green. It's just green. What's happening right now? You don't have anything else to say about it other than you like the green?

HERMAN. Well ...

BELLYWAX. *(Tilting his head as he looks at it.)* What's that on top of it? Is that some type of ranged weapon?

AMADO. A weapon?

BELLYWAX. Yeah. Stand right here. Tilt your head like this. *(The three of them all tilt their head together as they look at the canvas.)* See? It does! Looks like a catapult of some sort.

HERMAN. Ooo or a crossbow!

BELLYWAX. No, it's much too big for a crossbow.

HERMAN. Well, I meant a big crossbow!

BELLYWAX. Oh yeah, I think you're right. A big crossbow.

HERMAN. Very big!

AMADO. No. It's not a crossbow.

BELLYWAX. Ha! Told you it was a catapult!

AMADO. No. It's not a catapult either. It' not a weapon of any sort.

HERMAN. 'ow do you know, sir?

AMADO. Because I designed it. This is the blueprint of the secret project I've been telling you both about for weeks. We're building this.

HERMAN. That looks like a mighty powerful weapon you're building yourself there.

BELLYWAX. He's already told you that it's not a mighty powerful weapon. Why don't you ever listen!? It's a secret project weapon.

HERMAN. Oh, right.

AMADO. No. NO! It's not a weapon! I've already said this! Are all the castle guards like you two? I really hope that both of you are just anomalies to the human race.

HERMAN. *(Awkward pause.)* You say we got animals runnin' about, sir?

AMADO. Dismissed. You're both dismissed. Go away.

BELLYWAX. Is there anything we can do for you before we leave, your majesty?

AMADO. Just make this moment end. Please.

HERMAN. Sure thing, your majesty! *(Bellywax and Herman exit. Amado returns to the easel and tilts his head again – second guessing his design. Maybe it does kind of look like a weapon? Taxman enters carrying a document and lets out a depressed sigh.)*

AMADO. Why are you still here? Didn't I say that you were dismissed? *(Noticing Taxman.)* Oh, Richard Taxman. It's you. Wow. You look awful. Like you lost a bet on a jousting tournament and then fell off your horse on your ride home and while you were on the ground, a 10-year-old child kicked you in the shins with sandals made of iron.

TAXMAN. That's ... very specific, your majesty.

AMADO. It happens to the best of us. So, how did it go in the Sharlay region?

TAXMAN. It's been a terrible day, your majesty. And I'm a terrible tax man.

AMADO. *(Sympathetic.)* What? Noooo.

TAXMAN. I tried. I really did, King Amado. But they just

continue to refuse. And this Corbin Moss fellow, he touched my satchel. He pulled it and ran his fingers all through it. And then he gave it to his friends, and they all fondled my satchel as well. It was a disgrace.

AMADO. And his friends refused to pay too?

TAXMAN. I have never seen so much refusing in all my lives.

AMADO. You know, I've been over the numbers time and again since I first came to the castle. This land is very prosperous. Everyone is well paid, and those who want to work can always find work. The problem is that no King before me has ever put an appropriate tax level in place. With the current rate, I'm afraid it won't be long before the treasury runs dry. Come. Let me show you something. *(He pulls Taxman to the easel.)* Take a look at this canvas. This is the secret project I've been working on. *(Taxman begins to tilt his head to look at it but Amado grabs his head and positions it upright.)* No, please don't tilt your head like that. Just look at it straight on.

TAXMAN. It's so beautiful. I'm sorry, sir. You have your secret projects to fund and I'm failing you.

AMADO. Have faith, Taxman.

TAXMAN. Maybe you'll say I can chop their arms off if they refuse again?

AMADO. What?

TAXMAN. Or pluck their eyebrows out one hair at a time?

AMADO. Well ... I do like the creativity, but I don't think that's the right answer.

TAXMAN. I know, I know. I've just never been refused in this way before. Sometimes when I'm out collecting they say, 'I do not have money at this time, but I can make arrangements'. Or they say, 'How bout you take my child instead' or something of that kind. But a refusal like this? It makes me want to take extreme measures.

AMADO. What's that you're holding?

TAXMAN. Oh this? It's a license.

AMADO. A license for what?

TAXMAN. This license allows me to walk in a straight line.

AMADO. Huh?

TAXMAN. I know what you're thinking, but the way he talked, he made it sound like it would help me with my job. So I purchased this straight-line travel license from him.

AMADO. From who?

TAXMAN. Deke Harvey. He was at the Moss residence when I returned there. One moment they were all refusing and then... I'm not sure how it happened ... but the next thing I know, Harvey had talked me into buying this license, wind insurance, satchel insurance, and car insurance. I don't even know what a "car" is.

AMADO. I'm wondering if this Deke Harvey has a license himself.

TAXMAN. I think he does, sir. He looked like the type of man that walked in straight lines often.

AMADO. No. I mean a license to sell insurance. Did you ask him if he was certified to sell?

TAXMAN. I didn't think about it.

AMADO. Well, if he isn't then you will be entitled to all your money back.

TAXMAN. Really? That would be wonderful. Although, his rates weren't all that bad.

AMADO. *(Snapping sense into him.)* Taxman!

TAXMAN. You're absolutely right, sire.

AMADO. I want you to check up on Deke Harvey's credentials. If the Moss family and his friends in the Sharlay region do not submit what's due by the time you return, I will begin arranging their arrests.

TAXMAN. As you wish, sire! *(The two of them begin a soft devious laugh. It builds to where they are eventually both insanely laughing like villains.)*

AMADO. *(Stops abruptly.)* Enough.

TAXMAN. Right. Sorry, your majesty.

End of scene.

ACT ONE
Scene 5

The top of Mount Jeremy. Some wind sound effects as the scene opens is a nice addition.

At rise, Corbin, Henri, and Duncan enter.

CORBIN. *(Out of breath.)* Henri ... I thought you said ... this place ... was close.

HENRI. His office should be right around here somewhere. I hope he's home.

CORBIN. We just climbed a mountain. A mountain! Now ... you're telling me that we may have just... wasted our time?

DUNCAN. It all has to do with the Mystic Mandate that originated during the Thousand Psychic Wars. *(Flips through pages of his law book.)* Here it is. *(Reading.)* "Any being claiming to be a sage, soothsayer, or mystic must take residence in a hard to reach destination, such as atop a steep mountain, in a dark creature-infested cavern, or inside an active volcano, or else his, her, or its reputation and credibility shall be ruined." From what I understand, not many have chosen the volcano option.

CORBIN. I wish you would have mentioned this sooner. *(Jeremy the Sage enters. He wears a robe and is carrying a staff. He is immediately startled and screams at the sight of his visitors.)*

JEREMY. Ah! What's going on here? You nearly gave me a heart attack.

HENRI. We've come looking for a profoundly wise sage.

They say one lives nearby. Are you he?

JEREMY. Do you have an appointment?

HENRI. I knew I forgot something.

JEREMY. Oh, no worries. I already knew you were coming. I am a sage after all. Jeremy the Sage. What can I do for you?

CORBIN. You knew we were coming yet you were startled and screamed when you saw us?

JEREMY. A scream of joy.

CORBIN. And the heart attack we nearly gave you?

JEREMY. A … heart attack of joy, dear friends.

DUNCAN. Amazing. I've never met a living sage before. Will you sign my book?

JEREMY. Gladly. *(He signs Duncan's law book.)*

HENRI. It's an honor to meet you, Jeremy.

JEREMY. Oh, please. No need for the informalities. You can just call me Jeremy the Sage.

HENRI. Right. Of course. Jeremy the Sage. We've come to you for advisement. Please tell us if fate is on our side. We are about to embark on a very dangerous mission and before we go through the trouble of doing it, we'd really like to know if we will succeed or not.

JEREMY. And what is this mission?

HENRI. You see, there's a new king over our region ... out in Sharlay ... and we feel that his new tax is unfair, and we'd like to have him removed from power.

JEREMY. I see.

CORBIN. *(Aside to Jeremy.)* Look, Jeremy .... *(Corrects himself.)* Jeremy the Sage. Come over here for a sec. Here's the thing. I didn't want to bother you at all, but my friend, Henry, insisted that we visit you. Just tell him something to make him happy, and we'll be on our way, okay?

JEREMY. Right, right. I gotcha. Let me handle this. *(Addressing everyone as he goes into a trance-like state.)* So, you've come up with a plan to overthrow King Amado. You've gathered a team of supporters. A speaker, a writer, a law keeper, and a ... Hackus?

HENRI. That's my name! Henrietta Hackus!

JEREMY. Your plan is to make it look like the King is dead. Poison, am I right?

DUNCAN. That's right, sir. *(They are all listening intently now due to his accuracy.)*

JEREMY. And your writer is a lady. Smart. Charismatic. With access to the castle. Ah, so she's the one doing the deed. She's going to gain access to the palace. Try to seduce the King into having a drink with her and then poison his glass when he's not looking. But wait, that's not poison. Ah, of course, you don't want to actually kill the King. You're all too good-natured for that. This is just something to make him look dead long enough for ... long enough ... hold on. *(Screams dramatically.)* Ah! No! Something isn't right. This lady friend of yours. She's going to fall.

HENRI. Oh no! Does she fall into a pit? Is it a pit of spikes?

DUNCAN. Does she fall into the pit or is she thrown into the pit?

JEREMY. *(Still trancing.)* She falls. It's not a pit though. No, wait. Oh, she's okay. She's okay, everyone! *(Sigh of relief from everyone.)* She's perfectly fine.

CORBIN. Great! You here that? Everything goes perfectly fine then. See, Henry.

JEREMY. Well, can I make a suggestion?

HENRI. Yes, please.

JEREMY. *(Hands Henri a business card from his robe pocket.)* This is my sister's card. Now, before you say anything, I just want you to know that I don't normally give references, but my sister is a well-trained warrior.

DUNCAN. *(Reading the card.)* "Lenny the Dragon Slayer"?

JEREMY. Yeah, she's a dragon slayer too.

DUNCAN. But there's no such thing as dragons, right?

JEREMY. It's merely a title. Now, look. You can go with this poison thing if you like, but my suggestion would be to contact my sister, Lenny. She's a ferocious fighter. Perhaps, you can arrange a duel between her and this King. I assure you she'll win.

CORBIN. What? No. We don't want to go through all that trouble. That would draw too much attention. You say the fake poison will work, right?

JEREMY. *(Aside to Corbin.)* I gotta be honest here. I'm not really a sage.

CORBIN. But I just heard you lay out our entire plan without knowing any of the details beforehand.

JEREMY. I'm just a really good guesser, okay. I've always been good at it. Ever since I was a kid.

CORBIN. But isn't that technically what being a sage or fortune teller is all about? Making good guesses about the future?

JEREMY. There's no wisdom involved with what I do. At all. I just pulled all that out from under my robe, hoping I'd be right. Now, listen. You really need to get in touch with Lenny. She's well respected and she'll give you a good price. Her wife has been real pushy lately. You know ... threatening to kick her out if she doesn't get more contracts, so you'd both be doing each other a favor.

CORBIN. No, thank you. We'll go with the poison. *(To the others.)* Come on. Let's go. We've already wasted enough time.

HENRI. *(Looking at the business card.)* It looks like this Dragon Slayer lady lives right near us.

CORBIN. We aren't going to hire this guy's sister. Okay? We will go with the original plan. You heard him say that everything would turn out fine.

DUNCAN. But he did suggest that Lenny might be a good alternative.

CORBIN. Noooo. Come on.

HENRI. Thank you for your time, Jeremy the Sage!

DUNCAN. It's been an honor. *(Corbin, Duncan, and Henri exit.)*

JEREMY. *(Calling out to them as they are walking off.)* Remember. That's Lenny with two N's and a Y. There's another Leni that spells his name with one N and an I. But honestly, he's also a good warrior. So, really either one would be fine. But then again, the Leni that spells his name with one N and an I died about three months ago, so if you do come across him, you should probably just run away. As fast as you can. My uncle used to always say "Necromancy is never fancy". And my uncle hated rhyming, so you know it's gotta be true!

 End of Act One.

ACT TWO
Scene 1

Back in the throne room of Amado.

At Rise, Guard Bellywax is standing in the throne room with Estelle, who is pacing nervously. There's an awkward silence, and then ...

BELLYWAX. King Amado is very excited about this, Miss.

ESTELLE. Wonderful.

BELLYWAX. He told me there's only three times in your life when you're guaranteed to have your name in the newspaper. When you're born. When you get married. And when you die.

ESTELLE. Indeed.

BELLYWAX. So, he takes advantage of opportunities like this. You know, where he doesn't have to die. Or get married. He's even more excited about this than the secret weapon project he's currently building.

ESTELLE. What? He's building a weapon? Tell me about it.

BELLYWAX. Well, it's got some greenish areas along the sides with various ... shades of ... now wait a second. This is a secret project. I'm not supposed to be sharing that information with you.

HERMAN. *(Enters with attitude.)* Ebeneezer Bellywax!

You filthy thief! You guilty little squirrel-witted dung chaser.

BELLYWAX. Have you gone mad? Can't you see we have a guest?

HERMAN. I know it was you.

BELLYWAX. Me what?

HERMAN. I 'ad a full plate of scones sitting in the break room and you stole 'em.

BELLYWAX. I did no such thing.

HERMAN. Wipe those lies off your lips, you baboon-faced bandit.

BELLYWAX. How dare you?

HERMAN. I said what I said.

BELLYWAX. And I said I didn't do it.

HERMAN. Oh yeah? Well, I 'ave one eyewitness that says 'e saw you take 'em. All of 'em.

BELLYWAX. Well, don't you think perhaps you should get a witness with two eyes. It would make your accusation much more credible.

HERMAN. I also 'ave some pretty suspicious evidence against you.

BELLYWAX. Yes, but wouldn't "ugly" suspicious evidence be a bit more damning?

HERMAN. *(Observing Bellywax's collar.)* Ah! Look at that. On your collar. Crumbs!

BELLYWAX. Are you calling me a liar?

HERMAN. That would be too kind of a word for what you are!

ESTELLE. Excuse me, guys. Don't forget. You have a guest.

BELLYWAX. Terribly sorry, miss.

HERMAN. Our emotions get the best of us sometimes.

BELLYWAX. *(Beat.)* Maybe you.

HERMAN. Alright! That's it! *(Herman grabs Bellywax and tries to wrestle with him; Bellywax fights back.)*

BELLYWAX. Hey! Let go of me!

HERMAN. No. You let go of me! *(King Amado enters carrying a basket of wine bottles.)*

BELLYWAX. *(Notices King Amado.)* Stop, stop, stop. His majesty is here! Stand up straight and get that dumb look off your face. *(They both get back into their guard poses.)*

HERMAN. Your face is dumb.

BELLYWAX. Shhh!

HERMAN. And smells.

AMADO. *(To Estelle.)* Miss Avery! What a thrill it is that you're here. When they told me that you wanted to do a story on the King's wine ... well, I must admit, at first, I took offense. I thought they meant "whine", like I'm a big whining baby or something. But then they explained that you were referring to "wine" as in drink.

ESTELLE. Oh, sorry for the miscommunication. Yes. I'm interested in doing a story about the Royal winery.

AMADO. Excellent! I've just returned from the palace cellar and I've brought what looks like three of our best. Surely you can't review the King's wine without tasting a sample. And ... *(Notices the Guards are still standing in the room.)* Oh, I see that you've met Herman and Ebeneezer. Our ... most trusted royal guards. I hope these two were good company in my absence.

ESTELLE. Yes. A very ... spirited duo there.

AMADO. *(To Guards.)* Thank you, sirs. You're dismissed.

HERMAN. *(To Bellywax.)* She called us spirits. What you s'pose she meant by that?

BELLYWAX. You probably frightened her with all your screaming. *(They exit.)*

AMADO. So, how shall we begin? Perhaps a few standard opening questions? Like, King Amado, how did you get so handsome? Or what will it take for me to receive a kiss under the waning moon?

ESTELLE. I beg your pardon?

AMADO. Oh, you can come off it. It's just the two of us now.

ESTELLE. This is an interview about the winery?

AMADO. The King's winery? You really want to continue with such a silly charade. I know why you're here.

ESTELLE. You do ...?

AMADO. Miss Avery. You're not the first lady that has deceivingly made her way into the palace to try to win my charm. I'm afraid good looks can be such a burden sometimes.

ESTELLE. You're mistaken, your majesty. The Kingdom Press has instructed me -

AMADO. Right, right. Of course, that would be true if it were ... *(Looking for the right word.)* ... true. But do you really think you would've been allowed into the castle if we hadn't already contacted your employer? They know nothing of your coming here.

ESTELLE. *(Loss for words.)* Well ... I ...

AMADO. The King's winery? No doubt a fine subject considering it hasn't been covered in years from what I understand. But there's a reason for that. It was shut down because too many of the workers were drinking on the job. What're the odds, right?

ESTELLE. I see that you're a man of great intellect. *(Pretends to give in.)* You've ... figured me out.

AMADO. There it is. There's the truth. And you know what? The truth is attractive. I like you, Miss Avery.

ESTELLE. I'm very fond of you too, King Amado. The

wine interview was just a clever ploy to get you to share a drink with me.

AMADO. Clever doesn't seem like the right word. That implies your plan worked.

ESTELLE. In a way it did. You are going to share one of your bottles with me, right?

AMADO. *(Reveals a wine bottle from the basket.)* You'll have to forgive me. I don't know much about wine. I just grabbed the first three I saw with interesting pictures on the label. As one does, amiright? Alright, here we go. This one has a picture of an evil horse on it.

ESTELLE. Why do you say the horse is evil?

AMADO. Look at his face. He's angry. His eyes are slanted like he's mad at the World.

ESTELLE. You don't think good horses can be angry from time to time?

AMADO. I suppose they could be. *(Reading off the label.)* It says here ... "The best and ballsiest bottles from Bellywax Vineyards." Well, how bout that? The guard that was in here earlier is a Bellywax. I wonder if he's related.

ESTELLE. Shall we drink?

AMADO. You really are a striking woman, Miss Avery. *(Reveals two wine goblets from the basket and pours.)*

ESTELLE. *(Under her breath.)* More than you know. *(Causing a distraction.)* Oh, what is that other bottle I see? Behind you? In the basket there? Is that a limited-edition Lion's Roar Special you have there?

AMADO. I'm not familiar with that brand.

ESTELLE. Maybe you should ... turn around and look. Just to be sure. You never know. I do adore the Lion's Roar Special.

AMADO. Sure thing, Miss Avery. *(He focuses on the basket and looks through the bottles.)* Let's see here. It doesn't say Lion's Roar.

ESTELLE. *(Under her breath.)* Alright. Just one pill should do the trick. Here we go.

AMADO. What was that?

ESTELLE. Oh. Uhhh ... pilllllll ... lowwww peak! Yeah, that's what I was trying to think of. Do you have any pillow peak white blends back there?

AMADO. *(Revealing a wine bottle.)* This one has a picture of a mermaid on it. Or did you mean this one? *(Pulls out the other bottle.)* No, that one has a picture of a grassy meadow with a giant in the background. Eh, he doesn't look so menacing, all itty bitty on a bottle like this. *(Waves with his finger to the bottle.)* Well hello, little giant. Not so threatening now, are ya? *(Looking closer.)* Oh wait, no. That's not a giant. It's a windmill. But no. No Pillow Peak White blends in this batch.

ESTELLE. Wait! Don't turn back around yet.

AMADO. Why?

ESTELLE. I ... have a surprise. Just a few more seconds.

AMADO. Oh. Okay. I like this little game.

ESTELLE. *(Under her breath.)* Come on. Hurry up ... dissolve ...

AMADO. So turn towards you now?

ESTELLE. No! Not yet!

AMADO. Oh my. This is exciting.

ESTELLE. 3, 2, 1 ... aaaand okay. You can turn back now.

AMADO. Well, alright. *(He excitedly waits for a moment.)* Okay. I'm ready.

ESTELLE. Ready for what?

AMADO. The surprise.

ESTELLE. Oh. Uhhh ... *(Awkwardly.)* surprise!

AMADO. Sooo ... the surprise was you ... saying surprise?

ESTELLE. Mmhm. Shall we drink?!

AMADO. Absolutely. Cheers. *(They clink their glasses and are about to drink when Leon enters.)*

LEON. Good news, sir. Your letter has been delivered to Werner and the secret project matches your design blueprints perfectly.

AMADO. You have the most awful timing, Leon. I was about to share a drink with this lovely damsel.

LEON. Oh, I'm sorry. They didn't tell me you had a guest.

AMADO. Miss Avery. Please allow me to introduce Leon Crumbles.

LEON. How do you do, Miss?

ESTELLE. Fine. Thank you.

AMADO. Leon here is our palace jester.

ESTELLE. Oh, how exciting!

AMADO. You know, I still don't fully understand this term "jester". I mean, the word "jest" isn't a commonly used verb nowadays. Did you jest today? Did you jest yesterday? Yes? No? Maybe I'll jest later? I jest don't like it. Can we try calling you something else?

LEON. What would you prefer, your majesty?

AMADO. You're here to crack jokes, right?

LEON. Sometimes. I guess.

AMADO. Right. How bout we start calling you Leon the Cracker?

ESTELLE. Or maybe Leon the Jokester?

AMADO. Oooo! Leon the Jokester! I like it.

LEON. I don't mind jester, really.

AMADO. Oh, I got it! Leon the Joke Specialist! Now tell me that doesn't sound important.

LEON. It's a little long.

AMADO. You'll get used to it.

ESTELLE. Do you always have your court jester ... I mean your Joke Specialist ... reporting on secret projects?

AMADO. Of course. They're the best people to report on classified information. Everyone sees him as a fool. Look at him. No one would believe anything he says if he ever tried to ruin the surprise of my secret project. *(To Leon.)* Leon. I'd like to travel to Werner tomorrow to see the progress myself. I know. You feel like you've been on a fool's errand. *(Offers his poisoned glass of wine to Leon.)* But you've done well. Here, Leon. Take this glass and Join us in some fine wine.

ESTELLE. No!! Don't drink that one! *(She frantically reaches to block Leon from grabbing the wine glass and falls on the ground ... as predicted.)*

AMADO. *(Helping her up.)* Are you okay, Miss Avery? That was a nasty fall. I'm sorry. I didn't think you'd mind if Leon had a little. I was only going to give him the one glass. There will be plenty more for us.

ESTELLE. I mean ... he just... he looks like he has a... uh... *(The first thing that comes to her mind.)* ... a wine allergy. Is that right?

LEON. Well, I don't quite know. I've actually never drank wine before. I do take a lot of vitamins though, so I have a great deal of confidence in my immune system.

ESTELLE. But ... but ... I can see it. Yes. Come here, King. Let me show you. *(Pulls Amado closer to Leon.)* See. His skin's texture. Oh yes, it's perfectly clear that you should steer away from any wine offerings. Do you see it too, your majesty?

AMADO. *(Looking close at Leon's face.)* Well ...

ESTELLE. Trust me. It's there. In the flesh. Literally. Before becoming a journalist, I worked in the medical field and you better believe that I've seen wine allergies go very badly.   There was one gentleman who had such a bad allergic reaction that he fell into a coma and then, when he woke up, he walked sideways for a full year and thought everyone's name was Irving.

LEON. In that case, thank you, sir. But I think I'll pass.

BELLYWAX. *(Enters.)* King Amado. Here to report that Leon has returned from Werner, sir, with good news regarding your ... *(Noticing Leon is already in the room.)* ... oh, I see Leon has already presented himself.

AMADO. Ebeneezer! I was just talking about you. *(To Estelle.)* Estelle, this is the one I mentioned earlier who is from the Bellywax family.

ESTELLE. You don't say.

AMADO. *(Shows the bottle to Bellywax.)* Here. Take a look at this. Was this wine bottled by your family?

BELLYWAX. Indeed, sir. My father has been making wine ever since I can remember. He worked in the King's vineyard for many years until it was shut down, but then he ventured off on his own. Looks like you have a bottle of the Grand Bellywax Evil Horse Pinot Noir in your hands there.

AMADO. Evil Horse, you say? *(A look to Estelle.)* Are you sure he's not just an angry good-natured horse?

BELLYWAX. Absurd. All horses are evil, sir. Everyone knows that. It's in their genes. The Evil Horse Pinot is the best product in the Bellywax line, in my opinion.

AMADO. By all means, this goblet is yours. In honor of your family's long service in the Royal Vineyard. *(Gives the poisoned glass of wine to Bellywax.)*

BELLYWAX. Oh wow. Really? *(About to drink.)*

ESTELLE. Wait! Uhhhh ... Don't' drink that. I think ... I think that you may have ... *(The first thing that comes to her mind. Again.)* ... a wine allergy?

AMADO. Another with wine allergies?

BELLYWAX. Oh, I'm not allergic to anything, Miss. Plus,

I've been drinking wine ever since I was in my mother's womb. *(Drinks the poisoned wine.)* Ah, still has that Evil Horse taste. Flavorful. Just like liquid hooves. *(He collapses to the floor after a beat.)*

LEON. Oh dear! He just collapsed like a stack of potatoes.

AMADO. Whoa!

LEON. That wine must have a lot of horsepower.

AMADO. *(Takes a moment to appreciate Leon's joke.)* Haha, good one, Leon. But no, this must be the allergic reaction.

LEON. Good thing I didn't touch the stuff.

AMADO. What do we do, Miss Avery?

ESTELLE. I'm sorry?

AMADO. You said that you dealt with this sort of thing before you were a journalist.

ESTELLE. Yes, of course. I ... uh ...

LEON. *(Feeling for a pulse on Bellywax, but doesn't know where to check so he touches random parts of his body.)* I don't feel a heartbeat. I think his allergy killed him. Or is this like that coma you mentioned earlier?

AMADO. I hope not. I don't think I could ever get used to being called King Irving. He should have listened to your warning.

ESTELLE. Yes ... well ... I think I must be going. I've got to ... start piecing together an obituary ... you know ... just in case. Ebeneezer Bellywax was it?

AMADO. Yes.

ESTELLE. Okay. Just ... keep monitoring him to see if he comes out of it.

AMADO. Well, what's your medical advice? How do we know if he's dead or in a coma?

ESTELLE. He'll start smelling dead in a day or so if he's dead. Gotta go! Byyyeeeee. *(Hastily exits.)*

LEON. This is going to be a tough call, sir.

AMADO. I know. He already had a dreadful stench to begin with.

End of scene.

ACT TWO
Scene 2

Back at the Moss residence.

At rise, Corbin, Cayly, and Henri are pacing in the room, waiting to hear if Estelle succeeded or not.

HENRI. How do you think it's going?

CORBIN. We won't know anything until she returns.

CAYLY. We put together a solid plan. That Estelle is a quick thinker.

CORBIN. Still. I wish you would've waited for us to return before sending her off like that.

CAYLY. I had no idea when you'd be back. And she was really excited about it. She said that she'd always dreamed of being on a dangerous spy mission.

CORBIN. Perhaps if we hadn't had to trek up the side of mountain to visit a sage, we could've been here to work things out with you.

HENRI. It was for the best.

OSWALDO. *(Enters.)* So, you did visit a sage?

HENRI. Yes. He was amazing.

CORBIN. He wasn't a sage, okay. He was just... a really good guesser.

CAYLY. Well, what all did he say?

CORBIN. Not in front of Oz.

OSWALDO. Did he tell you if your plan to dethrone King Amado was going to fail or not?

HENRI. What?

CORBIN. Cayly! You told him?

CAYLY. I never said a word. I swear it.

HENRI. I knew it! You have the gift. Corbin, I've been telling you for years that your son is unique and special. And here it is, revealed for all of you. We didn't have to climb that mountain after all. Oswaldo is a wise old sage himself.

OSWALDO. *(Playing along.)* Yes, Henry. It is I, the wise "old" sage. And I have a wise prediction for you.

HENRI. You do? Well, tell me. What is it?

OSWALDO. I predict... that these walls are terribly thin and I can hear everything you people say when I'm in my room.

CAYLY. Oz! You should've told us that you knew.

OSWALDO. I didn't see the point.

CORBIN. Just know that our plan was formulated with the best of intentions.

OSWALDO. Is this something that might be written in the history books one day? What are the consequences if your plan fails?

CORBIN. According to the sage, Estelle is going to be fine. It should work out.

OSWALDO. Did he say your plan is going to be fine or Miss Avery is going to be fine?

CORBIN. Well ... Henry, he did say the plan was going to work out, right?

HENRI. "The walls are terribly thin... hear everything from a bedroom."

CORBIN. What're you doing?

HENRI. Oswaldo gave a most cryptic prediction. Just give

me a few more minutes. I'm pretty good at figuring these things out.

DUNCAN. *(Enters the front door.)* Corbin. Henry. I've got news.

CORBIN. What is it?

DUNCAN. I just saw Deke Harvey being arrested by the palace guards.

CAYLY. They must know. Just call the whole thing off!

DUNCAN. No, it's not that. They were saying something about wanting to see his license to sell his products.

CORBIN. And?

DUNCAN. The certificate he provided them had expired and he had no evidence of renewing.

HENRI. What? That's horrible. *(Reveals a document from his pocket.)* I really hope it was still in good standing when he sold me the color blue. *(Looking it over.)* Wait a second ... that doesn't even look like Deke's signature.

CORBIN. They took him to the palace dungeon?

DUNCAN. I suppose so, sir. It took six guards to bring him in.

CAYLY. Oh, no. Don't tell us that he tried to fight back. I'm sure that only made it worse.

HENRI. Deke never seemed like much of a fighter.

DUNAN. No, he wasn't fighting. Just talking. He managed to convince four of the guards that they didn't have the correct style and colour of armour to be making arrests. By the time the fifth guard approached, the first guard had figured out that he'd been duped and joined back in. He then said to both of them, "We all know that tadpoles swim on an empty stomach. If a license expires, that's nothing more than tadpoles swimming on a full stomach, am I right?

CORBIN. What does that even mean?

DUNCAN. I don't know, sir. But the way he said it made

both the guards nod in agreement and go walking off. Finally, a sixth guard approached with his ears covered like this ... *(Imitating the guard.)* ... so that he couldn't hear Mr. Harvey speaking, and he managed to arrest him and bring him to the palace.

CAYLY. What can we do?

HENRI. Do you think they'll torture him and make him reveal everything about our plot?

CORBIN. No, Henri. They would have no reason to even question him about any of this. It's a bit unfortunate, but totally unrelated.

DUNCAN. Have no worries. I've already decided to represent him in the King's court. I'll get him out of this.

CAYLY. Thank goodness! *(Knocking at the front door.)*

ESTELLE. *(Outside door.)* It's me! Estelle! *(Corbin opens the front door and she enters.)* This is all just a total mess!

CORBIN. What happened?

CAYLY. Did it work?

HENRI. Did the King drink the sedative?

ESTELLE. Well, someone drank it. But it wasn't the King.

CORBIN. Who?

ESTELLE. One of the castle guards. Bellywax, the King called him.

OSWALDO. What? My friend across the river is a Bellywax. His dad is a guard. Did you poison my friend's dad!?

CAYLY. Let's not get over excited here.

HENRI. Oh no, oh no, oh no, oh no. This is all going so terribly wrong. What're we going to do?

CORBIN. Just let me think. *(To Estelle.)* Can you still get into the castle? I know that we can't try the poison thing again, but maybe something.

ESTELLE. I overheard him say that he's about to travel to Werner for a few days.

CORBIN. Oh no. We may have missed our only opportunity then.

DUNCAN. You do know there's only one road that leads to Werner, right?

CORBIN. Yes. The Nightingale path. Straight through the Cuenga Forest.

DUNCAN. *(To Henri.)* Henri. Are you thinking what I'm thinking?

HENRI. All you can eat pigeon wings tonight at the Feathered Tavern?

DUNCAN. No. The card.

HENRI. The card. The card?

DUNCAN. Lenny the ...

HENRI. *(Reveals Lenny's business card from her pocket.)* Dragon Slayer!!

CORBIN. No!

OSWALDO. You're friends with a guy that calls himself a Dragon Slayer?

CAYLY. Who is that?

CORBIN. It's a lady. A fierce warrior apparently. She's the sister of that crazy mountain guy.

HENRI. Lenny is a dueller. And Duncan's been doing some research and according to his book, the King must accept all duels. Right?

DUNCAN. Well, only if the challenger recites the proper phrase. *(Flips through his book for the passage.)* Yes. It's written here. If he says this phrase and this phrase alone, then a King cannot back down and must accept.

CORBIN. Okay, but we're not out for blood here. JEREMY. said his sister was a master warrior. We're only trying to make it look like the King is dead just long enough for Estelle to publish a story. We aren't really trying to kill him.

CAYLY. What if you request this warrior to not use deadly weapons? Maybe just knock the King out for a bit.

HENRI. And when the King's people see him fall, they won't know if he's actually dead or not. It could work.

ESTELLE. And if it helps, I can write up the story ahead of time and that way as soon as he falls, it can immediately be sent off to the printers.

CORBIN. Well ... I suppose ... it's all we got at this time.

ESTELLE. But we just need to make sure everything happens as it's written, so that I don't have to make any last-minute revisions.

OSWALDO. It might be your last hope, dad.

CORBIN. Henri. Go get us a Dragon Slayer.

End of scene.

ACT TWO
Scene 3

On the Nightingale path. Outdoors scenery (can be implied). Horses are heard trotting.

LEON. *(Offstage.)* Woh. Wooooh. *(The horses neigh and stop. Guard Herman enters stage right holding his stomach followed by Leon.)* Guard Herman, you don't look well. Are you sure you're alright?

HERMAN. Yes. Well ... *(Almost begins to puke.)* Oh, please don't let the other guards see me like this.

AMADO. *(Enters.)* Why have we stopped again? *(Observes Guard Herman.)* What're you doing?

HERMAN. I can't 'elp it, sir. It's the 'orseback riding. All that bouncing and 'opping about. Gets to the pit of my belly every time. And I think my 'orse in particular is an angry fella. 'e keeps looking at me funny.

AMADO. Not angry. Evil. All horses are evil. There're always plotting something.

HERMAN. 'orses are evil?

AMADO. Yes. It's in their genes. Now, hurry it up.

HERMAN. I didn't notice my 'orse was wearing any jeans. *(Lenny enters dressed in full armor and carrying a staff.)*

LENNY. You there! I'm looking for the one they call King Amado.

AMADO. I'm the King here. Who are you?

LEON. Be careful, sir. She's armed. Shall I get the other guards?

LENNY. My name is Lenny the Dragon Slayer.

AMADO. Never heard of her.

LENNY. Perhaps you know me by one of my other names. I'm also known as Lenny the Dragon Destroyer, Lenny the Dragon Fighter, Lenny the Dragon Soul Crusher, and Leo the Cringe of the Sixteen Misfits.

LEON. Oh, I've heard of the Leo one.

AMADO. Have you really trained in fighting dragons?

LENNY. I'm an expert in the art of dragon slaughter.

HERMAN. I don't quite understand that. Why would you train so 'ard to fight a creature that doesn't exist?

LENNY. The words of a silly mortal. A dragon could come into existence at any moment. You were once nonexistent yourself.

AMADO. Fair enough.

LENNY. Now, let's get on with it.

AMADO. Get on with what?

LENNY. Our duel. *(Henri quickly enters carrying a torn piece of paper.)*

HENRI. *(Aside to Lenny.)* Lenny. Wait. Duncan says you have to say this phrase to the King exactly as its worded here or he can decline. Remember. We need him to accept, so make sure that you say the words in that exact order, okay? *(Quickily exits.)*

AMADO. Who was that hiding in the bushes? What's going on here?

LENNY. Never mind him. Prepare yourself, King Amado, for you will not be able to resist these words once I say them to you. The sacred passage enticing all noblemen who hear it. Are you ready?! *(Reads from the paper.)* "I challenge you to a duel."

AMADO. Hold up. That's the sacred passage?

LENNY. Did it strike fear into your soul, mortal?

AMADO. I was just expecting something a little more … poetic is all.

LENNY. Now, let's get on with it.

AMADO. You want a duel then? With me?

LENNY. You heard correctly. *(Henri enters carrying a sword.)*

HENRI. Wait! Estelle says you have to use a sword. The article she wrote references a sword, not a staff. We gotta be exact with the words she wrote in order to speed things up with the announcement. So give me that staff, and take this sword. *(Takes the staff and gives Lenny a sword. Estelle quickly enters.)*

ESTELLE. No! I said it's the King that has the sword. Lenny needs to keep the staff. Remember. No deadly weapons.

HENRI. Oh, sorry! Here, Lenny. Give me the sword and take the staff back. *(Gives Lenny back the staff and takes the sword and then runs off stage.)*

AMADO. Miss Avery! Is that you? Are you a part of this too?

ESTELLE. Well … gotta go. Byyeeee! *(Quickly exits.)*

LEON. I've got a bad feeling about this.

AMADO. No worries, Leon. I've got it under control. Very well, Lenny, my Dragon Slaying friend. I accept your duel. *(Corbin enters.)*

CORBIN. *(Aside to Lenny.)* Lenny, please remember. No killing. Just knock him out.

AMADO. What is going on? How many of you are hiding in those bushes??

LEON. Oh, Corbin! Hey! I was hoping I'd run into you. I've

got a witching clock that needs some repairs. Is it okay if I drop it off sometime tomorrow?

CORBIN. Of course! My boy has been wanting to see a witching clock up close. Um ... I do kinda have a thing going on at the moment though ... soooo how bout next week?

LEON. Oh, sure. No problem.

AMADO. Corbin? As in Corbin Moss, the Time Repair Specialist? The one who has greatly upset Richard Taxman? You have others with you too, I see. Is this the full group that refused to pay my new tax outlined in decree one-one-seven? *(Estelle and Henri enter.)*

CORBIN. We'd love to chat about that, your majesty, but you seem a little occupied at the moment.

AMADO. Oh, this will be quick.

LENNY. You underestimate my talents, King.

AMADO. But don't you know? I'm a classically trained Dragon Slayer Slayer. I've been enhancing my skills in fighting dragon slayers my entire life.

LENNY. What? That's ... I was not prepared for such a mighty warrior.

CORBIN. No, Lenny. He's bluffing. He's trying to put doubt into your head.

AMADO. I'm royalty. Don't you think that if dragons ever came into existence, that a King would do his best to own one? And in owning one, I'd need to know how to subdue all threats toward my dragon, hence needing to know how to battle incoming dragon slayers?

LENNY. I ... perhaps you and I were meant to battle then.

AMADO. Look. Lenny was it? Maybe there's a way to handle this without all of the exhausting swings and dodges. Please allow me to introduce Leon. He's the palace mystic with powers to see into the future.

LEON. What? I am?

AMADO. Yes. You are.

LEON. Oh right. I am!

AMADO. Now, tell us, if we were to fight this duel today, which one of us would win?

ESTELLE. No, he's lying. Leon is the court jester! I mean... joke specialist.

AMADO. *(Laughing.)* Do you hear that! I can't believe she bought it! You? The jester? Oh, Estelle. You said it yourself. Would I really send a jester to handle my classified projects?

CORBIN. Well?

ESTELLE. Well? I don't know.

AMADO. Now, Leon, I ask again. If we fight this duel today, which one of us will win?

LEON. *(After a brief moment, he begins to go into a fake mystic trance.)* I see it. The weapons are clashing. Over and over. Lenny uses his brute strength with every strike. One of them makes the King stumble to his knees. Lenny moves in for the critical blow, but the King gracefully dodges out of the way. And with Lenny's back to him, the King prepares the Gah Toe Mighty thrust manoeuvre – the award-winning tactic taught to all Dragon Slayer Slayers. Oh, the brutality! Lenny didn't see it coming. Please ... please! I can't watch anymore.

LENNY. *(Very nervous to hear the outcome.)* Tell us who wins... without the gory details.

LEON. *(Exhausted.)* The winner will be .... *(In his best announcer voice.)* King Amado!

LENNY. What!! Really? I guess there can only be one victor. I've fought many battles, and this is one that will stay in my memory for years to come.

AMADO. This is unexpected. You're such a brave warrior.

Lenny shall forever be a name of honor in my Kingdom.

CORBIN. Wait. That's it?

AMADO. The mystic has declared the winner by seeing into the future. What more do you want?

CORBIN. But?

LENNY. I'm sorry I failed you. He was a good opponent. And now I must be on my way. *(Exits.)*

AMADO. Now, we all have business to discuss. But first I have something important that I really need to say. *(Beat.)* You're all under arrest. Guards take them to the palace! *(The rumble of guard's feet is heard as the lights go to black.)*

End of scene.

ACT TWO
Scene 4

Back in Amado's throne room.

At rise, Taxman enters. He is alone in the throne room carrying a handwritten letter and his satchel.

TAXMAN. *(To his satchel.)* Ah. My legacy. My old faithful. My trusty satchel. We've had good times together, old friend, but I'm afraid our journey is over. It will be a difficult task to recover after being such a disgrace to his majesty and this Kingdom. I'm turning in this - my resignation letter. Yes. I'm resigning from my tax collecting duties. How can I not? To fail at my job is like a dagger being thrust through my heart. *(Reconsiders.)* Well, not exactly like that. But it's close. And maybe not my heart, but more like my left shoulder? You know, that's my weaker shoulder. That's why I carry you on the other. So it would hurt a little more in that one. And let's go ahead and say that the dagger is probably dull, so it wouldn't quite go all the way through my shoulder. Less blood that way. So, to rephrase that, to fail at my job is like a DULL dagger being repeatedly thrust into my left shoulder. *(Reconsiders again.)* You know, thrust still seems like a strong word. Okay, let's try this again. To fail at my job is like a DULL dagger repeatedly ... bumping against my left shoulder. Yeah, yeah. It builds a good solid soreness that way. That's precisely how I feel. Sore. And, of course, dear Satchel, this means that you'll have to resign as well. Oh, so many memories! I can still fondly remember the first time you were placed into my hands by grandpappy Telly Taxman. That look in your straps. I could tell that you could see the adventures that lied ahead. And adventures we had, old friend. *(Deke enters with his hands bound.)*

DEKE. Where's the exit to this place? I gotta get outta here!

TAXMAN. Hey! What are you doing here?

DEKE. Oh, I'm sorry. I ... uh ... I thought this room was a dungeon. My mistake.

TAXMAN. Where are the guards that were watching you?

DEKE. Well, they left me alone. I sold each of them a song title and now they're all rushing down to the Minstrel's Gallery to set up royalty payments.

TAXMAN. This castle doesn't have a Minstrel Gallery?

DEKE. That's okay. The songs don't exist either, but maybe, just maybe they'll be inspired to write them now, since they already own the rights.

TAXMAN. You did that thing with your words again, didn't you?

DEKE. What thing?

TAXMAN. You do something with your voice to make people listen. But what you say is just garbage. Still, they listen.

DEKE. Garbage!? Are you kidding me? If garbage only came in three flavors, would a minstrel really sing a song about it?

TAXMAN. I don't suppose so. Wait ... see there. You did it again. How do you do it?

DEKE. *(Hesitates but then...)* Alright, Taxman. Come here. Look. I'm a salesman. And they teach that little maneuver in the Salesman Guild. It's a little trick called "sensatone". Only about five per cent of those in the guild are ever able to master it. It's a secret trick you do with your voice to make anything you say sound convincing and reasonable.

TAXMAN. Even when it's nonsense?

DEKE. The less sense it makes the better. Just remember, every duck has a pair of legs, and every pair of legs has a set of ducks.

TAXMAN. *(Nods in agreement)* Very true. Please. You must teach me. I came in here to leave my resignation letter for the King. But if I had your skills ... if I could do this "sensatone" trick ... well, I could be the best tax collector this land has ever seen.

DEKE. Well, by the looks of you, it'll take a lot of practice, my friend. But you can get there. For now, you should consider not resigning.

TAXMAN. *(Attempts to use sensatone.)* Well ... even a man with hairy toes can carry a flag to a party. Am I right?

DEKE. What? That's ridiculous. *(Realizes.)* Oh. Right. Yeah. I see what you did there.

TAXMAN. No good? Not enough nonsense? Ah, I'll keep working on it. This is fun.

AMADO. *(Enters with Leon.)* Richard Taxman! Victory is ours! *(To Deke.)* And you. Who are you?

LEON. That's Deke Harvey, your majesty.

AMADO. Deke Harvey? What ... what are you doing in here?

TAXMAN. We were just having a bit of a chat, sire. Why are you back so soon? I thought you were travelling to Werner today.

AMADO. I was. But we encountered your rivals from the tax revolt.

DEKE. Corbin Moss?

AMADO. Yes. Oh. You were a part of that too, weren't you? No matter.

TAXMAN. You arrested all of them?

AMADO. Yes. Did you know this went far deeper than just refusing to pay the new tax? They actually wanted me dead.

DEKE. Well. Only slightly.

AMADO. What do you know?

DEKE. I know that no one likes the fact that you imposed a new decree on your citizens. And I know the only way for you to be removed from power is for there to be an announcement of your death.

AMADO. So, they were trying to kill me then.

DEKE. Not exactly. You see, only a public announcement of your death across the kingdom is needed to dethrone you, so really you just had to look like you were deceased long enough for an article to be published.

AMADO. Leon! Go retrieve the prisoners.

LEON. Yes, sir! *(He exits.)*

TAXMAN. You villain! Embracing such horrendous behavior is inexcusable! You tried to stage the death of his Majesty?

DEKE. Well, stages are meant for comedy and tragedy. Laughter and death. Without laughter, the unicorns will go into extinction. And without death, the unicorns will take control of the World, am I right?

TAXMAN. He's got a good point, sir.

AMADO. *(Also skilled in sensatone.)* But even baby unicorns are born with a pointy horn. Makes birthing that much more difficult. Extinction is inevitable, am I right?

DEKE. I've never thought of it that way. *(Realizes.)* Wait a minute. Did you just – Were you ever a part of the salesman guild?

AMADO. It might've been an early career endeavor?

DEKE. Bravo, your majesty!

HERMAN. *(Enters with Duncan.)* I couldn't stop 'im, your majesty. 'e was using fancy words like "evidence" and "barbarian".

DUNCAN. Not barbarian. I said law "librarian". My name is D. Duncan of the Sharlay Law Services and I'm here to represent Deke Harvey. I'm qualified, and I have evidence showing that he did in fact renew his salesman guild license.

AMADO. Oh, that's the least of worries at this point. Now, he's being arrested for the attempted staging of the death of the King.

DEKE. Well, there's no law against just "staging" a death, now is there?

DUNCAN. Actually, there is. But I submit that you have absolutely no evidence of this.

LEON. *(Enters escorting Corbin, Henri, and Estelle.)* Here they are, sire, as you requested. The leaders of the rebellion.

DUNCAN. Oh, dear.

AMADO. Corbin Moss. The lovely Miss Avery. And ... *(Doesn't know Henri's name.)* ... you.

HENRI. Henri.

AMADO. Deke here tells me that you were trying to fake my death so that I'd have my kingship removed.

CORBIN. That's right.

AMADO. And all it would take is a quick public announcement that I passed away? *(To Estelle.)* Is that where you came in, Miss Avery? That moment between us? Was it all just a game?

ESTELLE. I'm sorry. We weren't looking to actually hurt you or anything.

AMADO. Maybe not me. But I'm assuming my guard, poor Bellywax, was your doing. You know, when he finally woke up, he went and checked himself into a clinic for a wine allergy remedy. The thought of not being able to drink a good bottle of wine was too much for him to bear. Thankfully he wasn't walking sideways when he left out of here. And Mr. Harvey? What was your role in all this?

DEKE. I'm just a salesman.

DUNCAN. A salesman that has a fully renewed license, I might add, and shouldn't have been arrested in the first place.

HENRI. *(Reveals document from his pocket.)* Does that mean my purchase of the color blue is still valid?

DEKE. Of course. And a bargain, I tell you.

CORBIN. *(Finally had enough.)* Henri, what's that gonna do for you? Deke is a scam artist and ripped you off. I don't know why you can't see that.

DEKE. That hurts, Corbin.

CORBIN. It's true, isn't it?

HENRI. I know what you're thinking. And you're right. I may be dumb, but I know you're only saying this now because the situation is getting to you, and -

CORBIN. No, Henry. Look. I'm sorry to put it so bluntly. I just don't like seeing my friends scammed into buying useless stuff ... *(He takes the document from Henri and is about to rip it when something on it catches his eye.)* ... wait a minute.

HENRI. He just makes it all sound so enticing.

DEKE. Now, hold on one second. I've always given everyone fair prices. You're all making it sound like I'm some sort of villain here. I'm just a businessman, not a scoundrel. And every business transaction has fine print.

AMADO. Enough. Alright. You all admit to being a part of this, so therefore I'll give you several accommodating options.

CORBIN. Wait. This certificate! This is brilliant!!

AMADO. And fine options they are.

CORBIN. *(To Deke.)* Deke, I sincerely apologize for ever doubting you. *(To Henri.)* Henri! This is the best purchase you've ever made.

HENRI. What is?

CORBIN. This! Duncan, come here and look at this document. *(Points to an area on the document.)* You see that?

DUNCAN. *(Looking at the document.)* Oh. Is that really his signature?

AMADO. What's going on here?

CORBIN. Well, King Amado. Henry here purchased the color blue a while back from our good friend, Deke. She owns it. And according to this document, she's entitled to royalties whenever anyone displays the color, which also includes every shade of blue that you display in your castle.

TAXMAN. Royalty doesn't pay royalties!

AMADO. I'm afraid you're mistaken. Any such purchase that was sold and signed by this man, Deke Harvey, is not valid.

DUNCAN. This purchase wasn't signed by Mr. Harvey, your Majesty. It was signed by your predecessor, King Azul.

AMADO. Let me see that.

CORBIN. *(Hands Amado the document.)* And it clearly states that Henry is entitled to collect payments on anything that contains the color blue. Your castle is not exempt.

AMADO. Deke. You sold this to him? Where did you get it? Is it a forgery?

DEKE. Absolutely not! I attended King Azul's annual banquet years ago and he would always sign autographs at the event. I presented this certificate to him and he thoroughly looked it over and signed it.

AMADO. Leon, you were with King Azul before me. Is this really his signature? *(He gives Leon the document.)*

LEON. I'm afraid so, sir. It looks like he approved this

certificate.

HENRI. And as my payment, I'd like to receive every bit of coin from the decree one-one-seven tax that you've collected. From all the citizens. I am going to give everyone their money back.

CORBIN. So, you may arrest us now, but at least you won't be burdening the people with any more of this new tax of yours.

AMADO. This is ... unbelievable. Everything in here is blue. I mean, I could take it all down, or paint over some things but ... Oh, I don't know how I'll ever fund my secret project now. They've already begun construction ... if we stop midway ... I fear it will never get done.

ESTELLE. You can find some other way to build your secret weapon, but don't plan on it being paid for by the people.

AMADO. Secret weapon? Why does everyone keep using that word?

ESTELLE. That's what you're building isn't it? A greenish dangerous weapon?

AMADO. No, I'm not building a weapon. Show them, Leon. *(Leon turns the easel toward the others (and the audience) revealing a design for a school building drawn on the canvas.)* This is my project. This school building here. It's not a weapon. Unless you consider a good quality education a weapon. It's a new school being built over in Werner. Honestly, I don't know much about being a King. So, the first thing I did when I was crowned was listen to the complaints of you people. Number one was the lack of schooling opportunities in this kingdom. I do believe Miss Avery even wrote an article in the Kingdom Press on it. This would've solved that problem and allowed every child to receive a positive social education. Initial construction was started using the standard taxes, but it wasn't enough. I needed to enforce decree one-one-seven in order to finance the completion of the project.

HENRI. Corbin. With a new school, Cayly wouldn't have to teach Oz at home anymore.

CORBIN. I know, Henri!

AMADO. Leon says that this is indeed my predecessor's signature ... so I shall meet your demands and I'll have your payment delivered immediately.

CORBIN. Well ... perhaps ...

DOBSON. Greetings, your Majesty.

AMADO. Dobson! Look at you! Leon, told me of your progress. He didn't mention that you'd be visiting today.

DOBSON. He didn't know, sir. Just here to visit my mum for the day. I thought I'd come and see how things were in the palace while I was here.

HENRI. Dobson! You're alive!

DOBSON. I don't understand that question.

HENRI. We thought that you were arrested and being tortured in the castle dungeons?

DOBSON. Well, that's just silly. It's true I was arrested, but his Majesty offered me very accommodating options.

CORBIN. Options?

AMADO. Options, Mr. Moss. What age do you think we're living in? Torture? Come on.

DOBSON. His Majesty offered me a job in Werner as project leader. It has been an extremely rewarding experience. Not only am I getting paid, but the work I'm doing is for something great.

AMADO. Well, Dobson. I have some unfortunate news. Corbin and his friends are putting the project to a halt. You see, they have found a loophole and will be collecting all the funds received from decree one-one-seven and redistributing it back to the people.

DOBSON. But I'm the one that advised you on that decree.

I even named it. Henry, is this true?

HENRI. It wasn't my idea!

AMADO. You know, overall, I just don't get it. I don't blame you at all, Corbin. The problem is with the previous Kings. In the past, amenities were funded with treasuries of other lands we conquered, so there was never much of a tax on the people. At all. And now, for the most part, war and battles aren't so prominent anymore and I've inherited a land of citizens who are used to the idea that taxes are useless and only want to pay the bare minimum that was put in place years ago. I've seen the books. The economy is booming. The majority of citizens are wealthy and getting by fine. The tax laws indicate that the percentages are supposed to be based on the average income of everyone. It just doesn't make sense why they are set so low. The citizens are wealthy!

DUNCAN. I think the fish are the problem, sir.

AMADO. The fish?

DUNCAN. The Aquatic Citizens Act. It states that all fish in Kingdom waters are -

AMADO. - deemed citizens of the city! How could I have missed that?!

DEKE. Well, that explains it. You mix in the zero income of thousands of fish with the high income of us land walkers and that average doesn't look so hot.

AMADO. Well, I could just do away with the Aquatic Citizens Act and have the averages recalculated. So, it's possible I could bump the taxes to the appropriate levels without actually imposing a new decree. But that's still going to stir people up I'm sure. And ... either way you'll still be collecting your payment.

CORBIN. Henry. I think you were right from the beginning.

HENRI. I was?

CORBIN. Yes. Perhaps you could find another good use for

the color blue instead of taking money from this new school.

HENRI. I agree. Oswaldo and Cayly will be so excited!

AMADO. Of course, this doesn't change the fact that you tried to stage the murder of your King.

CORBIN. I hope you can see that this was all just a misunderstanding. If I had known what you were using the money for, I would have gladly paid. All of us would have.

ESTELLE. I was only given limited details when I wrote the article. And you're right, even if you overturn the Aquatic Citizens Act and recalculate the standard taxes due, it will stir people up. But maybe if you don't keep what that money is going towards a secret, I can explain everything in a new article. Put you in a good light.

AMADO. And ruin the surprise?

DOBSON. To be fair, your Majesty. It certainly got me on board once I knew what the project was.

ESTELLE. Exactly. Being King and leader of the land isn't about keeping secrets from citizens, even if they are pleasant ones. Be transparent and the people will support you.

AMADO. Tell you what, Henry. If you allow the castle immunity from collecting royalties on our bluish items, I'll remove all charges from you and your friends.

HENRI. Really?

AMADO. Duncan? I can do that, right?

DUNCAN. You are the King, sir.

AMADO. Okay, just checking. I'm still relatively new around here.

HENRI. Okay, sir. I declare that this castle is free from all fees on using the color blue!

AMADO. *(He lets out a devious laugh with a wildness in his eyes.)* Wonderful! It's done! Now, I can complete the construction of my massive mind-warping weapon! *(They all stare at him. Horrified.)* I'm only kidding. Leon, teach them a thing about humor, would you. *(To Estelle.)* You made a good point, Estelle. How about an exclusive interview for your new article?

ESTELLE. Yes! Let everyone know what you're working on. This will be great!

AMADO. I think it's time. How about over dinner tomorrow night? Join me in the palace dining hall. Without the wine this time though, okay?

ESTELLE. Of course.

AMADO. Now, all of you! Get out of my sight before I send you to the torture chambers! *(Deke, Henri, Estelle, and Taxman exit.)*

CORBIN. Hi. King Amado. Before I leave, I just want to thank you. I feel like an idiot. This could have ended much worse than it did.

AMADO. Very true. You know, this new school is going to have plenty of clocks throughout. I'll be in touch if any of them fail and need repairs.

CORBIN. Free of charge, sir.

AMADO. Well, that's nice of you.

CORBIN. And Leon, I'm available to work on your witching clock whenever you feel like dropping it off. Good day to you both.

LEON. See ya later, Corbin! *(Corbin exits.)*

AMADO. Leon. These recent events have got me thinking.

LEON. Do you think that's wise, sir?

AMADO. Very nice, Leon. Quick with the wit on that one.

LEON. It wasn't ... too much?

AMADO. On the border, but I'll let it pass. Just don't crack your jokes on me while others are around or I'll replace your jester cap with Guard Herman's underpants.

LEON. Of course, sir.

AMADO. Mr. Moss was right. This could have ended very badly. I mean, he was a rather civilized man. A little careless with his actions, but civilized nonetheless. Now, what if, it hadn't been Mr. Moss? What if some unruly citizen really came after me? With the wicked intention of actually murdering me?

LEON. Well, that would be tragic.

AMADO. Yes. I think, going forward, I need to acquire a body double. Someone to fill in for me if we ever sense there is a dirty plot lurking about. What do you think?

LEON. That might be a good idea, but if we -

AMADO. I knew it! Leon. I always just took you for a coward. I would've never thought that you would step up and volunteer for such a position.

LEON. What? Me, sir?

AMADO. Look at us. We both have the same build. Same features. Might have to do something about your face since you're not as handsome, but it's workable.

LEON.   But ... but wait! I tell jokes. I'm no King replacement.

AMADO. Think about it. Let's say there was a successful assassination on me. I mean, I can't think of anyone who would be more qualified to die in my place than you, Leon.

LEON. I can! I can make you a list!

AMADO. Are you saying that you wouldn't die for me?

LEON. Well ... I'm Leon the Joke Specialist. Remember?

AMADO. I'm kinda liking the sound of Leon the Body Double.

LEON. Joke. Specialist.

AMADO. Body. Double.

LEON. Joke. Speci-Ah-list.

AMADO. Body. Doo-blay. *(They continue to argue about being a Joke Specialist or a Body Double as the lights fade to black.)*

END OF PLAY

93

NOTES

(Use this space to make notes for your production)

BOBBY IS DEAD
by Marty Matfess

2M, 3W, COMEDY

Chris has been madly in love with his best friend Annie for years, but she's only been interested in dating everyone else but him. After Annie's recent break up with her boyfriend Bobby, Chris feels this may finally be what he needs to find his way into her heart, but just like that ... she's already moved on to another guy she met at a coffee shop. Being the good friend that he is, Chris has agreed to hang out with the new guy's visiting sister while they go out on a date. Oh, and let's not forget about Bobby. Turns out he's not taking the break up too well and Chris is now caught between an aggressive ex-boyfriend while having to keep new guy's sister company. A play about love, lust, and getting shot in the head.

HUGO SAVES CHRISTMAS…IN MAY!
by Steven Hayet

1M, 3W, COMEDY

For Maya Kaplan, Christmas is her life… and she hates every minute of it. As acting manager of a year-round Christmas store, Maya is force-fed jolly, subjected to hearing the same holiday songs on loop day after day. Fortunately, Maya's nightmare will be coming to an end in a few months as the store will finally shutter its doors to become a Starbucks. Or will it? Enter Hugo McGee, a longtime customer devastated to learn of the store's closing. Refusing to allow a local intuition to disappear, Hugo makes it his mission to raise the money and keep Yuletide Cheer open, despite Maya's objections.

www.ingramcontent.com/pod-product-compliance
Lightning Source LLC
Chambersburg PA
CBHW071437300726
48976CB00004B/1366